I0554275

Other Books by Gene Masters

Silent Warriors: Submarine Warfare in the Pacific
Operation Exodus
The Laconia Incident
The Wounds of Jonas Clark

Rich Vitelli Mysteries
The Dry Cleaner
True Believers
Bobby Doyle is Missing

All novels by Gene Masters, are available for order online and from multiple outlets.

Vitelli
in
<u>Venice</u>

A Rich Vitelli Mystery

Gene Masters

Published by Escarpment Press

Vitelli in Venice: A Rich Vitelli Mystery
Copyright © 2023 by Gene Masters

FIRST EDITION

10 9 8 7 6 5 4 3 2 1

ALL RIGHTS RESERVED

ISBN: 979-8-9867256-4-2

This book is a work of fiction. Names, characters, places, and incidents are either the product of the author's imagination, or are used fictitiously. Any resemblance to actual persons living or dead, events, or locations is entirely coincidental.

In accordance with the U.S. Copyright Act of 1976, the scanning, uploading, and electronic sharing of any part of this book without the express permission of the publisher constitute unlawful piracy and theft of the author's intellectual property.

This book may not be reproduced in print, electronically, or in any other format, without the express written permission of the author, except in the case of brief excerpts for publicity purposes.

Cover image ID# 243892717 Copyright © 2023 Shutterstock

Interior image ID#574139833 Copyright © 2023 Shutterstock

Escarpment Press
www.escarpmentpress.weebly.com
INDIAN LAND, SC

Chapter 1

Somewhere back up the Grand Canal, and past the Rialto Bridge, Donna Iams sat in a worn, padded, wing chair in a locked interior room. The unadorned walls were of peeling paint: cream-colored, ancient, and glossy, at least what was left of it. The ceiling was of white plaster, with spots of soot deposited here and there by long-gone candles. Now, the room was lit by what was once an elegant crystal chandelier with missing pieces; those that remained were yellowed.

She was still dressed in the same clothes she had worn at breakfast: blue silk blouse and pants suit. But at breakfast she had been smiling. Now she was in tears.

Someone speaking in strangely accented English had called up to her room at the Ca' Affascinante hotel early that morning. "Come quick!" he had said. "There has been an accident. Your husband has been hurt. He is in hospital and is asking for you. You *must* come."

She dropped everything and made her way downstairs and directly to the lobby, where two men were waiting. They looked ordinary enough: dressed, perhaps, like the resident working Venetians, in rumpled work shirts and brownish woolen trousers. One was tall and hefty, with a beefy nose, a pleasant, round face, and chocolate-brown eyes; the other much shorter — and lean. The shorter of the two — pockmarked face, gray eyes, and thin hawk nose — did the talking, his English with a strange — not Italian — accent. "Your husband needs you," he said. "Come with us. We have a boat waiting." They led her out into the late morning sunlight.

They said nothing as the boat pulled away and into the Grand Canal from the *Accademia* dock, and headed west and north, toward the Rialto Bridge. They had passed under the bridge before Donna thought to ask, "Where exactly are we going?"

"I said the hospital," the short man replied. "*Signore* Iams, he is there."

They were well past the Rialto when the big man pulled the boat well up into one of the side canals, turned left into yet another, and stopped at a long, concrete dock, or *fondamento*. "We are here, *Signora*," the little man said.

But instead of to a hospital, they had taken her here, manhandling her when she had resisted, having finally realized that she had been duped. "Tell me there was no accident, at least, and that my husband is all right," she pleaded.

"You can relax, *Signora*, he is fine, and you will both *stay* fine, just so long as both you and your husband, co-operate," was the answer.

"Cooperate?" she asked. "Cooperate how? With what?"

But neither man answered. Instead, they left the room, and locked the door.

Chapter 2

In the afternoon of the day before Donna Iams was abducted, Pam Vitelli was sitting in a vaporetto as the boat made its way up the Grand Canal. The day was gorgeous: sunny and mild, without a cloud in the blue Autumn sky.

Pam sat alongside her almost-new husband, Rich; they were holding hands and guarding their luggage, admiring the beautiful homes and *palazzos* that lined the waterway, their structures rising from the very waters of the canal, like some emerging Venus rising from the sea. Most of the buildings were marked with a black mold, and some had patches of missing stucco, exposing the powdery red brick beneath; yet there was something aristocratic and grandly elegant about each of them: grand old ladies sitting on old money. Each had its own landing, or a dock extending out into the canal. Securing pilings rose from the water; most were gaily colored (barbershop stripes seemed popular), some were at odd angles.

The Vitellis had flown into Rome overnight, having left Kennedy Airport in New York at 6:40 PM; then they flew east for eight hours and twenty minutes. Sitting up in coach, Pam had slept only fitfully during the flight. They were flying into the sun, so it was already 9:00 AM in Rome when they landed. By the time they cleared customs and made their way to the train terminal in Rome, it was almost noon. They were at Mestre terminal four hours later at just 4:00 PM (or 16:00, according to the clock in the terminal).

It was to be their ten-day, dream honeymoon in Venice. Pam Vitelli had been looking forward to it ever since she married Metro Police Lieutenant Richard Vitelli the previous March.

Oh, there had been a quick, three-day visit to New York City right after the wedding, but Pam hardly considered that a proper honeymoon. Between the hassle at Newark Airport (both going and coming), and the getting into, and then the getting back out of, the city, the two days and two nights at the Park Central Hotel hardly seemed worthwhile. By the time they had gotten to the hotel that Friday, and got to bed, Pam remembered that they were almost too tired to do much of anything. Now, she chuckled to herself, remembering how they more than made up for it the next morning.

Aside from the obligatory (for Pam, anyway) visits to the Metropolitan Museum, and the Museum of Modern Art (MOMA), the trip to New York was pretty much a bust. She thought that, right after the wedding, they might just as well have booked a room at the four-star Tecumseh Hotel back home in the city. They would have been far more relaxed and would have required a lot less sleep, anyway!

The exit from the train terminal had been right on the Grand Canal, and it was just a short walk to the vaporetto dock. The vaporetto was a kind of waterborne city bus: a long, wide boat, with lots of enclosed seating and plenty of standing room.

Pam was struck right off by the utter uniqueness of the place: the only highways were those of water, with no traffic patterns, just boats randomly passing one another. Nor was there an automobile or motor scooter in sight — there was not even a bicycle!

They had hauled their luggage to the dock. Unlike Rich, Pam was an experienced traveler, and had known enough to pack light. A suitcase on rollers and a backpack for each, made lugging the short distance to the vaporetto stop relatively easy. Of course, about half of what was packed in Rich's baggage was Pam's stuff. Pam waited with the luggage while Rich figured out which vaporetto they needed to catch, and bought tickets.

"Number two," he announced, "will take us all the way down the canal to our stop, the Accademia." They boarded the number two vaporetto, and headed up the Grand Canal. Neither had been to Venice before, and they delightedly absorbed all the exotic sights and scenes as their vaporetto made its winding way along the canal, stopping at various stations to load and unload passengers. As they passed them, they recognized many of the specific landmarks from the guide book they had both studied back home; but what they had seen in photographs and videos didn't do justice to the peculiar beauty of their surroundings.

As their vaporetto wound its way toward their destination at the other end of the city, they were given glimpses of the Venice its pedestrians knew by sighting down the various smaller canals that served just like side streets off a main highway. Each of these had its crossing footbridge. Unlike the buildings along the canal that seemed to rise unsupported out of the water, those that they glimpsed back inside the city were buildings built on what appeared to be more solid ground: homes, shops, and churches facing out onto paved squares and narrow streets.

Pam consulted her "Walking Venice" map, noting that there were three bridges that spanned the Grand Canal. The first had been the one opposite the train terminal. The upcoming bridge had to be the middle one of the three: the Rialto Bridge. Tourists, people just like themselves from all over the world, lined the railings and gawked down at them as their vaporetto made its way under the Rialto, and onward toward the third, and final, Accademia Bridge.

But before reaching the Accademia Bridge, the vaporetto wended its way to stop number twelve (the Accademia), just short of the bridge, where the Vitellis debarked. They searched a bit before they found their hotel, Ca' Affascinante. In the end, it was right there on the *Calle Dorsoduro*, number 724, where the "Walking Venice" map said it would be.

Besides being very close to the vaporetto stop, the Ca' Affascinante was also just steps away from not only the Accademia Museum, but also from the Linda Oppenheim Museum. In the Oppenheim was the show Pam had worked so hard to set up: Modern Works from American Museums, that exhibition now in its final week.

The hotel was expensive—even off-season it would normally cost three-hundred-eighty euros a night—but, her boss, Calvin Iams, had gotten them the special rate enjoyed by visiting museum staff. Even so, Pam was sure, their eight-day stay there was most likely costing her new husband a bundle. She has seen the pained look on his face when he saw the hotel's rates, but he assured her that they could afford it.

Chapter 3

The former Pamela Karns, widow of the late James Wagner, now Pamela Vitelli, was currently employed back home as the Assistant Director of the city's Metro Foundation Museum of Art. She had been hired for the job right out of Cornell University, where she had majored in Art History, and minored in Museum Administration. A scholarly paper she had written as an undergraduate had been published in the *Journal of Contemporary Art*. It caught the eye of the Metro Foundation Museum's Director, Calvin Iams, himself a well-known scholar of contemporary art. Iams was in the process of setting up the collection for the Metro Foundation Museum, and was looking for an assistant, an administrator who could handle the museum's day-to-day affairs. Pam was a bright young lady with a brilliant mind, one who could be hired at a bargain-basement price. Iams interviewed her while she was still a senior at Cornell, and was suitably impressed. He offered her the job upon her graduation, and Pam quickly accepted. She was thrilled to have landed any job in her field right out of school. Most of her fellow graduates with similar educational backgrounds were not nearly as fortunate. Some of them, she knew, were still working as baristas, or flipping hamburgers, back in their home towns.

Pam attacked her new job with the same intensity as she had attacked her studies. She had an eye for shrewd purchases of individual artworks, and had a knack for convincing private collectors that the museum would be a fine place to donate, or at least exhibit, their most prized pieces.

Two years after moving to the city, Pam met James Wagner, a young project engineer who worked for Dealey Enterprises. They dated for a year, and then married. Less than a year after their marriage, James consulted a doctor about a sudden onslaught of overwhelming fatigue, and bloodwork showed that he had been stricken with a virulent form of leukemia. A year of debilitating chemotherapy followed, but ultimately failed, and Pam became a widow just twenty months after her marriage.

She was devastated at first, but was never one to mope around and feel sorry for herself. Instead, she coped with her grief by turning to her faith, and by throwing herself headlong into her work.

Now, just over five years a widow, Pam had become the bride of Richard Vitelli, who was newly forty-five, and almost thirteen years her senior.

Her parents thought the marriage ill-conceived, and told Pam as much. They continued to think so even after they met, and even genuinely liked, Richard Vitelli. There was not only the age difference, but the fact was that he was a policeman, a man with a dangerous job, and they were loath to see their daughter bury another husband. No matter. Pam had set her cap for Rich Vitelli, and that was all there was to it. It didn't matter that Vitelli, while tall, had to fight to stay fit; had only a reasonably handsome face; had thinning, greying, hair; and was starting to go to seed. He had, or, so at least Pam thought, the most beautiful liquid brown eyes, the kind a girl just wanted to drown in.

Her brother, John, who had observed their romance from the start, noted that "the poor bastard never stood a chance." They had dated only three months before Vitelli proposed, and were married at St. Anselm's Church just a month later.

Chapter 4

After checking in, and settling into their room, Pam said, "I don't know about you, but I feel grungy. There's time for a shower before dinner, don't you think?"

"Okay," Rich said, "you go ahead. I'll just take a little cat nap."

Pam gave her husband a look, one that said "wrong answer." Rich saw her look and said, "But maybe I'll join you instead."

"Good idea," Pam grinned.

WHEN THEY WERE DATING, it quickly became clear that the chemistry between Rich and Pam was exceptional. Rich always thought she was a prize; he might describe his trim, athletic wife as handsome, rather than pretty, but just looking at her made his flesh tingle. Almost as tall as himself, Pam had an elegant oval face, clear skin, and a straight, slim nose. Her bright eyes were the color of dark, polished walnut. When they met, she had worn her auburn hair short and business-like, but he had persuaded her to let it grow to shoulder length. As he grew to know her, he found her classical good looks were matched with quick intelligence, sharp wit, and a throaty voice that thrilled him to the core whenever she spoke.

Besides, they were both Catholic, and had met at church, right after a Sunday Mass. Rich figured that perhaps God had planned for them to be together all along.

But Pam was also *very* Catholic. There had been plenty of passionate embraces, even some mutual bodily exploration, but Pam had made it very clear that until they were married, there would be no what she termed "hanky panky."

"And my biological clock is ticking, Rich Vitelli," she had said, "so you had better make up your mind soon. Time's a wastin'." And Vitelli had indeed made his mind up quickly.

Chapter 5

The 1,600-year-old city of Venice sits on the Adriatic coast at the top of the Italian peninsula. The city was built by waves of Italian natives fleeing first from the Visigoths, and then the Huns, in the fifth century, and later, in the sixth century, from the Lombards. These were hardy men and women who retreated to the northeastern saltmarshes, where even the barbarians refused to follow.

They discovered that by driving wooden piles close together into the squishy mud, and topping them with wooden planks and gravel, the now-stabilized ground would support all sorts of structures, including palazzos of stone and brick, and even magnificent churches.

They settled into a maze of some one hundred and eighteen islands, isolated together in a sheltered lagoon, separated from the Adriatic Sea only by a length of spits and barrier islands; the only access from the lagoon to the sea itself being three narrow inlets.

It was on the largest of these islands that the city of Venice was built. Venice evolved into a city of merchant mariners, their home a maze of conjoined canals, with a larger, wide, Grand Canal, snaking through its center. From the city's inception, travel throughout the city was exclusively by boat. The use of carts and pack animals for transport was entirely impractical then, just as automobiles and motor scooters are impractical today.

In its heyday, at the end of the thirteenth century, the Republic of Venice, *La Serenissima* – The Most Serene One – as it came to be called, was the richest city in all of Europe. It was the center of the continent's international commerce; its ships and sailors dominated the Mediterranean.

Today, though no longer nearly so rich, Venice is still a leading Italian cultural center, a major tourist destination, and remains one of the most beautiful cities in the world.

Chapter 6

It was already dark when the newlyweds finally deserted their hotel room, and it was time for a short evening stroll, or *passeggiata,* as the Italians called it. Since arriving in Italy, the October weather had been perfect: bright sunshine, warm days, and cool, clear nights. Tonight, with its gentle, salty, breeze off the Adriatic, promised to be no exception. They made their way across the Grand Canal via the Accademia Bridge, and walked north and east into the *San Marco* section, the heart of the city, and the site of St. Mark's, the city's magnificent ninth-century basilica, and its sprawling plaza. On the way, they passed between ancient buildings, structures elegantly moldering over time, each aging with a varying dignity.

Venice, the city, is very walkable, and it's almost impossible to get lost. There are signs prominently posted on the corners of buildings, pointing the way to the city's popular attractions. Pam need not have brought her map: the Vitellis more or less followed the signs pointing (with a black directional arrow) to "*San Marco,*" deviating only far enough to discover a *trattoria,* a cafeteria-style restaurant, where you pointed to what you wanted, and the servers behind the counter plated your selections. Far cheaper than a regular, food-made-to-order, sit-down, restaurant, the food was excellent, and the selection almost overwhelming. Coupled with a house wine, the Vitellis left the trattoria more than satisfied.

They then made their way to St. Mark's Square for a night-time looksee. Even in the evening darkness, the square was breathtaking: looming over the far end of the square were the spires and domes of *San Marco* herself, the magnificent basilica that lent her name to an expanse of open space lined with shops, offices, and studios. Completely out of step with the exotic church, was the overarching *campanile,* or belltower, a squarish spire that marked one corner of the square, a place for tourists to ride an elevator up and get a bird's eye view of the city.

Past the belltower, and next to the basilica, was the Doge's Palace, the offices and apartments that housed the *Doges,* the men who ruled the Republic of Venice from the eight to the eighteenth centuries. Its suite of offices and meeting rooms was still the center of *La Serenissima's* government. Across from a backing canal, separated by a short, covered bridge, known as the Bridge of Sighs, was a connecting prison. As they crossed the bridge to their cells, the Doge's prisoners could look out and along to the canal it crossed, for a last glimpse of the city. Legend has it that while crossing the bridge, the prisoners sighed, knowing they might never see the city again.

But the Doge's Palace was closed to the tourists at night, and the Vitellis would have to come back in the daylight to tour it.

The Vitellis made their way across the square and passed in front of the Doge's Palace to the *fondamento,* or landing, right on the Grand Canal, where two columns stood. One was topped with a lion, the symbol of St.

Mark, the other with a statue of St. Todaro. Todaro was the city's original protector saint, venerated as such before ninth-century Venetian merchants stole St. Mark's body out of Alexandria, and transported it to Venice.

Indeed, Pam and Rich had learned that most of the city's artifacts were stolen and transported from somewhere else. For example, the four horses above the portico of the basilica are copies; the originals, now housed in a museum below, were taken from the Hippodrome in Constantinople in 1204.

The two columns were transported from the East in 1000; there were originally three, each transported in its own boat. But one boat sank at dockside, spilling its column into the Grand Canal, and the Venetians thought it impractical to attempt to raise it. It's still there.

Having soaked up something of the city's atmosphere, the Vitellis found their way back to their hotel by following the signs pointing out the direction to *"Accademia,"* and the city's *Porso Duro* section.

Gene Masters

Chapter 7

It had taken almost a year of work, but Pam had finally pulled it off.

Calvin Iams had done the initial work, convincing the Museum of Modern Art in New York to participate in a collection of modern masterpieces from museums across the United States (including, of course, two gems, a Van Gogh and a Picasso, from the MOMA itself).

Pam had added to these, ten other modern masterworks, some of the cream of America's contemporary art museum collections. Pam had cajoled the directors of museums in Los Angeles, Seattle, Chicago, Miami, and Boston, to contribute major pieces from their collections to a month-long exhibition at the Linda Oppenheim Museum in Venice. The exhibition would be timed to coincide with the annual Venice Fall Festival of the Arts, and would be taken down at the festival's conclusion.

Pam's final task had been to assemble the individual pieces of art for the exhibit to be shipped to MOMA in New York for incorporation, and then see to their trans-shipment to Venice.

Iams was to take it from there, travel to Venice, and function as the exhibition's curator at the Oppenheim. Of course, the Metro Foundation Museum didn't have the budget to finance neither the round-trip to Venice, nor the

30-day stay at the Ca' Affascinante (even at the reduced rate for Iams). So, like the Vitellis, Iams and his wife Donna were travelling on their own dime. But Iams, at least, could easily afford it.

The job of an exhibit's curator required minimal effort. Pam, had, after all, done all of the hard part. Iams would simply see to the initial installation of the exhibit, a job actually done physically by the Oppenheim Museum staff, and then just check in daily until the end of the festival (which would be this coming Sunday); then, he would be responsible to ensure that the art was safely re-crated, and securely shipped back to New York.

It was an ideal arrangement, in that the Iamses had plenty of time to enjoy the city and its environs. And now, for the exhibit's last days, the Vitellis would be joining them. But—and this was clearly understood—Pam now had no responsibilities for the exhibit whatsoever. The Vitellis were, after all, on their dream honeymoon!

Chapter 8

The next morning dawned bright and clear, sunlight pouring into the Vitellis' room through the window that overlooked the pretentiously named *Rio di San Vio,* the narrow canal that linked the Grand Canal to the much wider Giudecca Canal.

Pam and Rich went to the small dining room on the first floor of the Ca' Affascinante for breakfast. (In Europe, there is the "ground floor" at street level, and the next level up is the "first floor.") They were dressed in American tourist casual: Pam in a bright yellow print blouse and tan slacks, Rich in a light blue knit golf shirt and khaki slacks. When they arrived, they found that Cal and Donna Iams had arrived before them.

"Pam and Rich," Cal called out, smiling broadly. "Welcome to Venice! Come and join us."

Calvin Iams was a short, round, man with a shock of white hair over a round face: a beardless Santa Claus in a European-cut, blue, pinstriped suit. Donna Iams was his physical counterpart, only shorter and rounder: a pleasant lustrous-white-hair-framed Grandma face, in a blue Italian-silk blouse, and not-quite matching blue, polyester pants suit.

"We will," Pam answered, smiling back.

Breakfast was from a variety of pastries and breads on a sideboard, along with fresh fruit and some cheese selections. After loading their plates, the Vitellis joined the Iamses.

After the two couples were seated, an attendant, a tall thin woman with a pleasant smile, and wearing a regulation black dress and white apron, took their beverage order: orange juice and cappuccinos all around. The cappuccinos were hot, and the orange juice fresh-squeezed and pulpy. "The Italians themselves are not into big breakfasts, but, otherwise, they certainly know how to eat well," Cal remarked. The others nodded in the affirmative.

"I know you two just got here," Donna said, "but I know you're just going to love Venice!"

"We love it already," Pam said, "at least what we've seen of it so far. This place is so incredibly exotic, and, as Cal says, 'the Italians really know how to eat well.' Our dinner last night was incredible—makes restaurant food back home seem so bland."

"It does indeed," Donna agreed. "Cal and I were first here as newlyweds, just like you two. Remember, Cal?" she smiled at her husband.

"I do," he replied, "so very well. Donna is fluent in several European languages, and her Italian, in particular, is superb—and *was*, even back then. So, naturally, we had to honeymoon in Italy. We went all over—Rome, Naples, Florence, Ravenna—but we fell in love with Venice. We were much younger then, of course, but not even the *Acqua Alta* dampened our enthusiasm for this city. We've come back—what—four times since, including this trip?"

Donna nodded, still smiling.

"Wait a minute, Cal, *Acqua Alta?*" Rich asked. "What's that?"

"Nothing you should need to worry about," Cal responded. "Used to be that the city would flood regularly—whenever the conditions were just right. The whole city would be under water; and the water came up pretty high—it would be knee-deep in St. Mark's Square. Apparently, it used to be a pretty rare event, but *Acqua Alta* began happening more and more frequently as the world ocean levels started to rise. Added to that, the city is sinking anyway, and has been for decades. So, I guess, the Italians had to do something. So, they installed this multi-million-dollar fancy system of barriers that rise up from the seafloor and dam off the inlets to the lagoon surrounding the city from the Adriatic. Supposedly, this new system works pretty well—but Donna and I have never been here when it was used."

"Let's hope it won't be needed while *we're* here," Pam said.

"Oh, I don't know about that," Donna said. "It was kind of fun, wasn't it, Cal? Besides, I don't think there really is a way to predict it. As I understand it, all sorts of stars have to align for *Acqua Alta* to happen."

Smiling, Calvin Iams nodded in the affirmative.

"Didn't faze the Venetians in the least, though, as I recall," Donna continued. "They were ready for it—set out all these raised platforms, making walkways throughout the city so people could walk about and not get their feet wet. As I said, it was kind of fun—certainly different, anyway. But I have to admit it was weird to see the floor of St. Mark's Basilica under a foot of water."

"Well, I'd just as soon we stay high and dry while we're here," Pam said. "Changing the subject, how's the exhibition coming along?" she asked Calvin Iams.

"Pretty well," he answered. "But space has been, and is, a problem. The staff was upset that they had to take down part of their permanent collection to make room for it. There's hardly enough room to display the Picasso adequately, and I'm having some difficulty with getting the lighting on the Van Gogh just right. It's a miracle, by the way, that you managed to convince MOMA to let them travel. Either painting is priceless, and I seriously doubted you would ever manage to convince them to let either out of their sight for a single instant. But you did it! You did an amazing job, Pam, in putting all this together."

Pam blushed at the compliment, and then Iams said to Vitelli: "Amazing gal, this little lady of yours. She could charm the stripes off a tiger!"

"That she could," Vitelli agreed. "Since these paintings are so valuable, I expect that the museum has added more security?"

"Hardly," Iams answered. "They are so lax I can hardly believe it. Seems everybody on staff has keys to the place. I'm just a visitor, and they gave me a set. And I can come and go as I please. Anytime. Day or night.

"There are guards," Iams continued, "but they are unarmed, even the two that patrol the place at night. Not even a nightstick. And I think the museum director, *Signore* Grimaldi, believes that the docents—all volunteers, mind you—are all that he needs to make sure nobody steals anything. And besides its artwork, the museum houses a load of pilferable items—thousands of valuable photographs stored in unlocked wooden cabinets, and small art objects displayed in simple glass cases. And, what with the Fall Arts Festival in full swing, the traffic through the place has been simply phenomenal—much more than normal, or so the staff tells me. Of course, I would like to think that our exhibit is largely responsible for that," Iams preened.

"All the museum staff has been complaining about the workload," Iams went on. "Seems that Grimaldi didn't think to add any additional people for the festival. So, as well-received and attended as this exhibition has been, I'm sure the Oppenheim staff will be more than happy to see the end of it—and me—Sunday night."

When they had almost finished breakfast, Donna Iams asked, "What are you two doing for dinner?"

"No specific plans," Pam answered. "Probably we'll go back to the magnificent trattoria we discovered yesterday evening. The selection was amazing, the food fantastic, and really reasonably priced!"

"Sounds wonderful," Donna said. "Mostly we have dinner in sit-down restaurants, and they're all *so* expensive! Cal and I had dinner yesterday at one of those places on St. Mark's Square, and while the food was superb, I do think we had to pay the waiter's entire year's salary for it!"

Cal nodded in agreement. "Quite a few hundred euros, anyway," he said.

"Well," Donna continued, "if you don't mind, Cal has one of those dreary meetings at the Oppenheimer this evening — arrangements for the traveling exhibit's closing this weekend — and I'm by myself for dinner. Would you mind terribly if I joined you two?"

"Not at all," Pam said. Rich thought that she sounded as if she actually meant it. He tried not to let his face reflect what he was actually thinking. *But I do mind! This is our honeymoon!*

"Lovely," Donna said. "Shall we say around seven o'clock in the lobby?"

"Sure," Pam answered. "Seven, in the lobby, it is. See you then."

Chapter 9

"I still don't see what you do in any of this stuff," Vitelli said. "It looks like so many random blobs of paint on canvas to me. Or, in this case, crayons scratched on paper."

Pam Vitelli sighed. She loved her husband, but was beginning to believe her efforts to school him in the meaning and beauty of contemporary art were hopeless.

They were in the Oppenheim, checking out the museum's collection and the travelling exhibition, and were currently viewing a painting by Pablo Picasso in the museum's regular collection; it was considered a twentieth-century masterpiece. The piece was entitled *Half-length Portrait of a Man in a Striped Jersey,* rendered, Pam had said, in gouache on paper. It was painfully obvious to Pam that her new husband wouldn't know gouache from goulash.

"It's surrealism, Rich," she explained patiently, "and probably a self-portrait of the artist himself. He frequently dressed in striped shirts like the one in the picture."

"Is that what *that* is? The stripes are crudely done—like some ten-year-old painted them. And what's with the way that the guy's head is all broken apart like that?"

"He's split up the face, making it multi-faceted, presenting it as a portrait in light and shadow."

"If you say so."

She sighed, and then they moved on to the next picture, this one a painting by Salvador Dali, entitled *The Birth of Liquid Life*. But their exchange went, again, much the same way as before.

"Now I think this guy Dali could really paint if he wanted to," Rich said. "But the figures are all out of whack—you know, distorted and all. Still, the detail is there, and very well done. Like he could be a good painter if he wanted to. He certainly is a better painter than that Picasso guy. Compared to this Dali, that guy couldn't paint his way out of a paper bag."

Pam was quickly becoming resigned to the fact that the man she loved was a troglodyte where contemporary art was concerned.

"All right," she finally said, "let's check out the traveling exhibit. Perhaps you'll see something there you'll like."

They moved to the rear of the building, where the exhibit that Pam had worked so hard to assemble had been set up.

There were, altogether, a dozen works hung on two permanent and two temporary walls. They had been placed close together as a matter of necessity; exhibit space in the Oppenheim was at a premium. Pam noted that Iams had set the exhibition up most effectively given the space constraints, and had used lighting masterfully. She steered her husband to the Van Gogh, one of two works that New York's Museum of Modern Art had sent:

The Starry Night. A village is depicted in darkness, with a single dark tree thrust up into a swirling blue sky filled with bright stars and a glowing yellow moon.

"I like it," Vitelli admitted, "but I couldn't tell you why. The colors are wild, and of course no night sky in real life looks anything like this. But, yeah, it's . . ."

"It's what?" Pam asked.

"Stirring. It's really stirring. But I could never tell you why."

Pam smiled. *Well, my dearest, that's a start, at least.*

After touring the exhibit, they went into the museum store. There they found Cal Iams, fussing with a tall, elegant-looking man in a blue silk suit. "You have to give the prints of the traveling artworks more exposure," he was saying to the man. "You have to understand that sales of these prints help fund the exhibit."

"I do understand that, *Signore* Iams," the man replied, "but the museum has to sell prints of our permanent collection as well. We have given you as much exposure as we possibly could. Besides, these prints are not like prints should be at all — the paper is good enough stock, but is embossed with those silly bumps to simulate brush strokes." He literally put his nose in the air. "Not quality prints at all! But anyway, have we not put a framed print of *The Starry Night* on display over the bin full of the other prints?"

"Not quality?" Iams questioned. "They are, *Signore* Grimaldi, *very* high quality indeed! One has to look closely to distinguish them from the originals. Look at the Van Gough print. The colors are almost as vivid and alive as the painting itself. It looks beautiful there, and has to be drawing buyers to the bin of prints. What about adding one or two more of the others?"

"Where, *Signore,* where?" Grimaldi said, apparently genuinely exasperated. "There is simply no more room!"

Iams shrugged in frustration. *A distinctively Italian gesture,* Pam Vitelli mused, *the culture is rubbing off on him!*

The two men sparred a minute or so more, and eventually a frustrated Iams threw up his hands in defeat. As Grimaldi withdrew, a suddenly smiling Calvin Iams spied the Vitellis and approached them. "Italians! There's no arguing with them when their minds are made up!" he said, as if in confidence. "Well, how are the newlyweds doing? Enjoying the exhibits?"

"We are," Pam replied, "or at least I am. I really like what you've done with the travelling works. You were right, the museum didn't give you much room to work with, but I think you've done a marvelous job with the space they *did* give you. And the job you did on the lighting of the Van Gogh is perfect. But I'm afraid Rich, here, is having a hard time accepting that art has moved on from the Baroque period."

Vitelli grinned. "Okay. I have no idea what a Baroque period is, but I suspect that means back when people painted pictures of things that looked like the things actually look in real life."

"Pretty much," Iams said, laughing. "I'll admit that most of contemporary art takes a trained eye. Pam, it appears that you have immersed poor Richard here into modern art much too quickly. Perhaps you should have started him next door at the Accademia. Start with the realists, and work up to the impressionists. They *do* have a few of the very early ones over there."

"Good idea," Pam replied.

THEIR QUICK VISIT TO the Accademia, just a few doors down from the Oppenheim, went much better, and Pam saw that there was definite hope for her husband's education in the arts after all.

There, Rich stopped and absorbed each exhibit, lingering longer at some than at others. He was particularly fascinated by *Vitruvian Man,* a drawing in pen and ink by Leonardo DaVinci. It showed the nude figure of a man centered in a circle, both standing upright and with arms and legs extended to show reach and stance. It was a small drawing, done on paper dimensioned akin to modern legal-size. Da Vinci had scrawled notes both above and below the picture, mysteriously written from right to left and backwards — a mirror image — as was his practice.

"Now *this,*" Vitelli exclaimed, "is really something."

Chapter 10

They spent the rest of the morning and the early afternoon just wandering around the city, the Autumn sun bright in a cloudless sky, the air cool and crisp. Using Pam's "Walking Venice" map for a reference, they were just wandering, getting a feel for the place, absorbing the atmosphere. Starting at *Plaza San Marco,* they toured the magnificence that was St. Mark's Basilica, tramped through the Doge's Palace, and, back outside, gazed at the Bridge of Sighs from the quay. They took the elevator up to the top of the *campanile,* and gawked out over the city.

Later, the Vitellis just wandered, walking their way through the city's back alleys and byways, even discovering, and crossing, the Rialto Bridge. They were continually getting lost, and then finding themselves in front of some landmark they recognized, a place where they could establish their exact location using Pam's map. They stopped only long enough to snack at a pastry shop, and Vitelli remarked, "Well, I guess we don't need lunch, now, do we!"

Pam laughed, a fleck of whipped cream still at the corner of her mouth, and nodded in agreement. "Guess not," she said.

"Wait a second," Vitelli said, "what just happened? All the shops are closing. Isn't it the middle of the day?"

"Siesta, silly," Pam answered. "Time honored tradition all over Europe. One o'clock to three o'clock, shops close, everybody goes home for a little nap."

"Sounds like a plan," Vitelli said, grinning. "How far are we from our hotel?"

"Not sure," Pam grinned back, "but it can't be more than twenty, twenty-five minutes at most."

THEY SPENT THE REST of the afternoon back at the hotel; in fact, it was almost six o'clock and getting dark outside, when Pam finally said, "Come on, lover. It's time for a quick shower and then get some clothes on. We're supposed to meet Donna downstairs at seven."

"Right," Vitelli replied. "Race you to the shower. I'll give you a head start."

"None of that. Get up and you get your ass out of bed. Come on now, we've got to behave like mature adults."

"Who said?" Vitelli questioned, but got up out of bed anyway.

Chapter 11

At seven sharp, the Vitellis were in the lobby, dressed for a casual evening in town. Pam wore a bright blue, print dress and a blue, cardigan sweater, Rich a fresh golf shirt and the same pair of khakis. But, by 7:20, Donna Iams had not yet showed.

"Wonder what's happened to her?" Pam said.

"Can't imagine," Vitelli answered. "But then I really don't know the woman."

"Well, I do, and it's not at all like her. I'm gonna call up to their room."

Pam went over to the desk clerk, a pretty young lady with her shining black hair tied back in a bun, and had her call up to the Iamses' room. No answer. She went back to where Vitelli was waiting, and said, "She's not answering the phone. I'm going to go up and knock on her door."

"I'll go with you," Vitelli said, and they both went up two floors to the Iamses' room and knocked on the door. No answer. Pam spoke out loudly, "Donna, are you in there?" Still no answer.

"Wait here," Vitelli said, and left. Minutes later, he showed back up, this time with the desk clerk in tow.

"Really, *Signore* Vitelli," she said, "I should not be away from the lobby."

"Understood. But as I said, this is an emergency."

The desk clerk opened the door, and all three went inside. The room was vacant. Vitelli nosed around, and noted that everything appeared to be in order: both Cal's and Donna's clothes were hung up in the closet, their respective toiletries carefully set out in the bathroom.

"Come, Vitellis," the girl said, "we really must not be here. I really must get back to the desk. Please come now."

"Okay," Rich answered, and the three of them vacated the room, the desk clerk locking the door behind them.

Back in the lobby, Pam said, "I wonder where she is, and what happened to her?"

"What about her husband?" Rich asked. "Wasn't the reason she was coming to dinner with us because the Iams will still be working at the museum? Let's go see what he has to say."

"Good idea," Pam said.

They walked down the street to the Oppenheim. There they found Calvin Iams, and Vitelli sensed right away that something was wrong.

"Donna was supposed to meet us at seven to go to dinner," Pam explained, "but she never showed up. That's not like her. She wasn't in your room, either. Any idea what might have happened to her?"

"Oh," an obviously agitated Iams answered, "I'm so sorry. There's been a family emergency. Donna has left— she's on her way back home. In all the hubbub, packing and such, I guess she just forgot to tell you."

"That's not true," Vitelli said to Iams, and when Pam flashed him an unapproving look for speaking that way to her boss, he turned to her and said, "He's lying, Pam, and you know it."

Then, returning his gaze to Iams, he said, "We were just in your room—the desk clerk let us in—and all her stuff is still there. Tell us what's really going on."

And then Iams broke down in tears. "They said that if I told anyone, they would kill her!" Calvin Iams sobbed.

Gene Masters

Chapter 12

Donna Iams knew she hadn't been there too long. The room was without windows, but there was a dingy skylight, and daylight still wafted its way through the haze. She sat down in an ancient, high-back, wing chair, covered in a faded purple brocade. Then she surveyed the other furniture in the room: a small table and a straight-backed chair, both of aged dark-brown-finished wood; a narrow bed—no linen, just a mattress; a grimy pillow, and a folded, blue, polyester blanket.

Her captors had not mistreated her in any way; when she had called out that she had to go to the bathroom, the big man came quickly and escorted her down a short hallway to a small room with just a toilet and a wash basin. There was, she noted, the same bad paint job as the room that had held her, and a grimy window high above the toilet. He respectfully closed the door, at least, and gave her some privacy.

"What are you going to do to me?" she asked in English, as the big man escorted her back to what she had decided was to be her prison cell.

"We will not hurt you," he replied haltingly in the same language, "so long as your husband, he cooperates."

"Cooperates? How? Cooperates with what?"

"Too many questions," he replied. "Soon I bring you dinner."

When she was back in the room, he closed and locked the door behind her, and she heard a bolt slide home.

About an hour or so passed, and she heard the bolt being withdrawn. Then there was actually a knock on the door, and she heard the big man say, "I have dinner." Only then did the door swing open into the room. The big man carried a tray of food into the room, and set it on the table. He said nothing after that, just turned and left the room. Once again, he closed the door behind him, and she heard the bolt slide home.

It occurred to her that she had not had anything to eat since breakfast, and that she was hungry. Dinner, as it turned out, was delicious. It was a pasta dish with creamy tomato sauce, and sweet Italian sausage. And there was red wine. *Perhaps they really don't mean to hurt me after all! Or are they literally just fattening me up for the slaughter?*

The reality of her situation could not be denied. Donna had been an occasional reader of detective novels, several of which described abductions just like her own. She knew full well, in every novel she had ever read where a person was kidnapped, the kidnappers never — *ever* — let their victim see their faces, not, at least, unless the ability to identify their abductors didn't matter, because they intended to kill their victim eventually anyway.

She had seen the men who had abducted her; their faces were indelibly etched into her memory. Donna shuddered, almost certain now that she would never be allowed to leave this room alive. Dead certain.

Chapter 13

"Who said?" Vitelli asked Iams. "Who, exactly, told you they would kill Donna?"

"A person with a weird accent on the phone . . ." He pulled out his phone, scrolled to a picture of Donna Iams, sitting in a grimy wing chair, looking distraught, and showed it to Rich and Pam. ". . . sent me this picture of Donna. She looks scared out of her wits. Then the guy said I'm to do exactly as they say, cooperate fully, or they would kill her."

"And what did they want you to do?" Rich asked.

"That he didn't say. What he *did* say was that they would contact me later, tell me exactly what they wanted me to do. And that I wasn't to tell anyone, especially not the police. He said they were watching me, and they would know, and if I *did* tell anyone—especially the police—then they would kill Donna for sure."

"They always say that," Vitelli said matter-of-factly. "But that's exactly what you should do. Go to the police."

"But how do you know they won't just kill her then?"

"Because she's the only leverage they have over you," Vitelli said, the voice of reason. "This has to be connected to the collection. The pieces in the Oppenheim exhibit are worth millions. These people are thieves, not murderers, and they're out to steal artwork."

"Easy for you to say. It's not your wife they've kidnapped."

"No, it's not. But I would like to think that if it *was* my wife, I would behave professionally enough to do the things most likely to get her back to me in one piece. Now tell me about this guy who contacted you. You said he had a weird accent?"

"Yeah. Spoke English with some sort of accent — not Italian. Slavic, maybe. From the Balkans, perhaps. Or Russian, even."

"Good. Now you have to tell the local cops everything you just told me."

"But they'll kill her."

"If they really mean to kill her, Cal, then they will anyway. Whether you cooperate with them or not. They will do what they intend to do, Cal, and that's already set in stone, no matter what you do."

"That's not very reassuring, Rich," Pam inserted. "Cal is scared. He's not used to dealing with these people the way you are."

"I understand that, hon', that's why he needs to let the professionals handle this." Then to Iams, "Let the local police handle it, Cal."

"Like the police back home handled Bobby Doyle's kidnapping?" Cal asserted.

That hurt. Back home, Bobby Doyle had been the star quarterback for the city's professional football team. He had been kidnapped and held captive by the disgruntled brother of a woman he had impregnated and abandoned. His abductor had every intention of killing Doyle. Vitelli almost found and freed Doyle, but a Russian Mafia kingpin got there first, and when his subsequent ransom demand was rebuffed, the gangster, in a rage, killed Doyle.

"Every case is different," Vitelli answered, fighting to appear unruffled, "and the person who kidnapped Doyle did so with the specific intention of killing him. Like I said before, if these guys really mean to kill Donna, then there isn't much we *can* do other than find her, and find her fast, before they can do that." *If they haven't already,* he thought, but was wise enough to keep that particular thought to himself.

"So, we should go to the cops," Iams said in resignation. "Would you be willing to help—help find her, I mean?"

"It's their territory, Cal. But sure, I'd be willing to at least ride shotgun with you when you report it to them. But look, Cal, the locals know the lay of the land, and have the best chance of finding the people most likely to be involved here before they can do anything to hurt Donna. I would like to be able to help with that, but I'm a duck out of water. I don't even speak Italian." *Besides, I'm on my honeymoon!*

"I don't speak it either—not very well, anyway—certainly not as well as Donna. The museum staff, they all speak English," he added, as if that had to do with anything. He stopped talking for a second or two, as if making up his mind. "Okay, let's do it. Let's find the cops and tell them."

Then, he said, "Wait! They said they'd be watching me!"

"I seriously doubt that," Vitelli replied, "but if they are, then all the better. They'll know they haven't scared you."

"But they sure as hell have," Iams said, sadly.

Meanwhile Pam had pulled out her "Walking Venice" map, and consulted it for a minute. "There's a *carabinieri* station on the south side of St. Mark's square. We can walk there from here in a matter of minutes."

"Okay," Vitelli said, "but you can stay here, Pam. We'll be back as soon as we can."

"Oh no you don't," Pam replied. "My Italian isn't all that great, but it's infinitely better than both of yours. I'm coming, too."

And so, the three left together, heading for the Accademia Bridge shanks mare.

Chapter 14

The brass plaque next to the door read: *Polizia Locale Sezione San Marco*. The door itself was multi-paneled and wide, covered with what looked like a shiny black lacquer, possibly centuries old. Or perhaps not. It was between two store fronts, the one to the left selling Verano glass baubles, the one to the right, high-end leather goods. If they weren't looking for it, the Vitellis and Calvin Iams might have passed right by without even noticing it.

Vitelli turned the shiny brass knob and the door opened inward, revealing a dimly-lit staircase leading up to the next level above the square. There was another door at the top of the staircase, that one dark brown. Vitelli leading, the three ascended the stairs. Another shiny brass door knob, another door opening inward, but this time into what seemed to be a brightly-lit office. About a dozen men and women (mostly men) in uniform, were there, at desks, writing, on the telephone, milling about. A young lady in a white dress shirt and black necktie sat behind a desk near the door and looked up as they entered. Vitelli noted that she was what any American would consider a typical Italian beauty: flowing shiny black hair, alabaster skin, chiseled features, and huge brown eyes.

"Buonasera, posso aiutarla?" she asked, politely.

"I'm sorry," Vitelli responded, "but my Italian is *'molto povero.'* Do you speak English?"

"A little," she responded, warily. "How may I help you?"

"We are here to report a kidnapping and a potential theft."

"Kid-a-napping?" she said, "po-ten-shall?"

"Una persona è stata rubata," Pam cut in, *"e 'potenziale.'"*

"Ah, una rapimento, e una potenziale furto!" the young lady said, then *"per favore, una momento."* Then she called out across the room, *"Tenente Giudice, per favore, vieni qui."*

A handsome young man, coal-black-hair, wearing a dark blue jacket complete with Sam Browne belt, white shirt, and black tie, approached them from a desk across the room. He wore trousers of the same dark blue material as the jacket, red stripe down the side. The young woman behind the desk stood as he approached, and Vitelli noted that, despite her wearing the same red-striped uniform trousers, her Venus de Milo figure was as totally beautiful as her face. When the officer arrived, he and the desk clerk conferred in rapid Italian. Then the young man addressed Vitelli and the others in impeccable English.

"Ah," he said, "I am Lieutenant Matteo Giudice. Sergeant Capello, here, (Vitelli noted that he looked at her with unabashed admiration) says you are here to report an abduction and a potential theft?"

"That's correct," Vitelli said, and Pam and Iams nodded in agreement.

"And who was taken?"

"My wife, Donna Iams," Iams said.

"And you are?"

"Calvin Iams. I'm the curator of the American art exhibit currently here at the Oppenheim."

"Very well, *Signore* Iams, I am pleased to meet you. And you are sure she was, what-do-you-call-it, 'kidnapped,' *Signore* Iams?" Giudice, asked, his almost black, dark brown eyes looking down an aristocratic nose, showing some skepticism. After all, tourists were reported lost every day, only to show up hours later, embarrassed and apologetic.

"I'm sure. The people who took her told me they would kill her if I didn't cooperate."

"Ah," he said. "Start from the beginning, then, *Signore*, and tell me everything." And so Iams did.

When Iams had finished, and after Giudice saw the video the kidnappers had sent, Giudice turned to Vitelli, "And so it was you, Detective Vitelli, who convinced *Signore* Iams to come to the police?"

"Of course," Vitelli responded. "Finding missing persons is what I do in America, and I'm familiar with how these people work. I advised Mr. Iams, here, that letting the police in on the case right away is the very best way to get Mrs. Iams back unharmed." Then he added, "Assuming, of course, they haven't killed her already." Both Pam and Iams, hearing that, grimaced.

"Grim," Giudice said, "but, unfortunately, accurate." He looked at Iams. "The man said they would contact you again. When they do, you must tell them that you will do nothing until they prove your wife is still alive.

51

And you must be firm about that. Only then will you consider doing whatever it is they want." Vitelli nodded in agreement.

Giudice turned to Vitelli. "Detective, I know you have no official status here in *Venezia,* but I would appreciate it if you would be available for, what-do-you call, consultation. I am new to this kind of case, and I'm sure I could benefit from what *Signore* Iams, here, says is your extensive experience."

"I'm happy to do whatever I can, Lieutenant," Vitelli said.

But Pam's expression mirrored her unhappiness with her husband's acquiescence. *Our honeymoon!* she thought, but she knew, in her heart, that he could not have said or done anything less.

"Excellent," Giudice said. "I am afraid there is not much we can do immediately, not until they contact *Signore* Iams again. But, in the meanwhile, I can get the word out on the street. If *Signora* Iams is still in Venice, one of our informants is bound to know about it."

Giudice handed Iams a notepad and a pen. "Write down your cell number for me, please, *Signore.* I will call you as soon as we learn anything."

After Iams had complied, Giudice gave his card to both Iams and Vitelli. "And here is my card. Call me anytime if you have any questions, or if there are any developments in the case."

When both men nodded their understanding, Pam sighed. *So much for our romantic honeymoon in Venice.*

Chapter 15

The Vitellis and Iams were back out on the square. Iams was lost somewhere in his thoughts, as Pam said to her husband, "I saw how you looked at that young lady in there."

"Come on, Pam, you can't be jealous. I'm old enough to be her father."

"So you are," Pam laughed, "and I never get jealous. Besides, I really can't say that I blame you for looking. She was absolutely gorgeous!"

Vitelli knew quite well that his best response to that remark was to just keep quiet.

"Anyway," Pam continued, "it's pretty obvious that there's something going on between her and the handsome Lieutenant Giudice.

"You think?" Vitelli said. "I hadn't noticed."

"You wouldn't," Pam said, and Vitelli, again, was smart enough not to tell her she was wrong.

Calvin Iams and the Vitellis started walking slowly back to their hotel. "Isn't there *something* we should be doing?" Iams asked.

"Like what?" Vitelli responded. "You heard the Lieutenant. There is nothing *to* do. Not until the kidnappers contact you again."

"But we could at least go out looking for her, couldn't we?"

"Look where, Cal? Be reasonable. We don't even know she's still in the city. And if she's anywhere, she's got to be inside a building somewhere, and none of us can see through walls. I'm afraid we don't have the slightest chance of finding her."

Iams said nothing more as they continued walking, staying silent until they reached the Accademia Bridge. Sensing his mood, the Vitellis had also maintained their silence.

When they reached the hotel entrance, Vitelli finally said to Iams, "When we go into the hotel, Cal, you need to go up to your room and try to get some sleep. At least, then, you'll be able to deal with something like a clear head when these people *do* get back in touch with you. And they will, Cal. And you must remember what Giudice said to you: You want proof Donna is okay before you assent to anything."

"I know," Iams said, but he remained an unspeaking, brooding, presence in the lobby of the hotel. Without further word, he left Rich and Pam in the lobby, and took the stairs up to his room.

"See you at breakfast, Cal," Pam called after him.

But Iams remained silent.

"Poor man is distraught," Pam observed. "In his shoes, you would be too."

"He is that," Vitelli said, "and, you're damn right, I would be too. But I would also do my damnedest to find, and cheerfully murder, the man who would dare do anything to hurt you."

Chapter 16

Breakfast the following morning was a somber affair. When Calvin Iams joined the Vitellis' table, it was clear that he had not spent a very restful night. He had taken a small amount of food from the serving table, but once seated, he turned his head away from his plate.

"Please, Cal," Pam said, "you have to eat something."

"I know," Iams replied, "but I'm just not hungry."

"Try eating something anyway," Pam chided.

He took a few bites, and even asked for *"Café Americano,"* when the attendant came and asked what beverage he would like.

"It's important that you go about your regular business, and act like nothing happened. Wait for them to contact you." Vitelli advised. "The kidnappers may or may not be watching, but they have to be confident that you're going to be cooperative."

"If they *are* watching," Iams replied, "then they will know we went to the police. I've been thinking about that all night, and I'm terrified that that was the wrong move."

"We've been through all that, Cal," Vitelli assured him, "and you *know* it was the only thing you *could* do. Besides, these people aren't fools. They will assume that you might well have gone to the police, and will have already planned around that."

"Okay," Iams replied, but he didn't sound very convinced. "Look, I've got to get to the Oppenheim. Meetings. Get ready to dismantle the exhibition, and the paintings ready for transport back home."

Iams then pushed back from the table and left the dining room.

But when Iams made to leave the hotel, and go to the Oppenheim, the desk clerk stopped him on the way out. "*Signore* Iams, a courier came by and left you a package."

Iams took the package and opened it. Inside was a cell phone, a charger, and a written message: "Keep this phone charged and on at all times. Do not alter any of its settings. We will use it to contact you whenever necessary."

Iams went back to the dining room, and was relieved to find the Vitellis were still there. He told them about the package he had just received.

"Okay," Vitelli said. "Not sure why they would send you a second phone — after all, they were able to contact you on your regular cell phone."

"They were. I assumed they got the number from Donna."

"You're probably right. But the second phone doesn't figure."

"The note did say *not* to alter any of its settings," Iams noted.

"Right." Vitelli thought about it, then said, "Bet they have the GPS set on it so that they will know where you are at all times. That's really very clever. Nobody else has the new number, either, and they know they can contact you whenever they want, and you'll be on tenterhooks waiting for their call. Moreover, they never have to contact you in person, ever, unless they want to. They are planning on your staying very worried and very scared, and are doing their best to maximize your anxiety."

"Well, they're doing a damn good job," Iams admitted.

Vitelli could not stifle a smile. "They're counting on it. But remember what Lieutenant Giudice said, and don't agree to do anything until they prove Donna is okay."

"I won't forget *that*," Iams said. He glanced at his watch. "Damn. I'm supposed to be in a meeting with Grimaldi, the museum director. This whole thing is making me crazy!"

"Go to your meeting. It's best that you make out as if nothing is happening, anyway. I'll see Giudice and tell him about the cell phone. I'm not that electronically savvy, but maybe there's a way they can listen in whenever they call you."

"Guess it might be possible, but I don't know about that stuff either. But go ahead and ask Giudice anyway."

"I'll do that."

Pam, listening, said nothing. *Guess we won't be seeing much of Venice today.*

Chapter 17

If Calvin Iams had little stomach for breakfast, Donna Iams had no difficulty whatever in consuming hers.

She was still locked away in the inner room, when one of her captors at least thought to knock on her door before unlocking it, and rolled a cart into the room. It was again the largest of the two men who had abducted her, and the cart contained an array of comestibles: pastries and bread, cheeses, sliced apples, strawberries, and even some cooked sausages.

"Not sure what you like for breakfast, *Signora*," the man said in his halting English. "I brought then many things. I know Americans like the big breakfasts."

"We do, actually," Donna answered in Italian. "And the things you brought look quite delicious."

The man smiled broadly. "You speak Italian! Wonderful! And there is coffee."

Donna hadn't slept well, certainly not still dressed in her street clothes, and on the narrow bed. But she was hungry, and she enjoyed a piece of pastry, along with some cheese and fruit. The coffee was Italian-style espresso — hot, thick, and strong — and Donna sipped it gingerly.

"You do not like the coffee," the man said, sounding disappointed.

"No," she replied. "It is fine. But Italian coffee takes some getting used to. And it must always be sipped, no?"

"Yes, *Signora*," he smiled. "Good coffee is for sipping."

"My name," she said, "is Donna. No need for the *Signora*."

"Okay, Donna. Call me Giorgio."

"That's not what the other man called you."

"No. Serb does not even know my real name, nor I his. Calls me Hulk. Those are our street names. Mine is supposed to mean that I am big and strong, or so they tell me. I think it really means that they think I am stupid. I *am* a little slow in the head," he admitted, "but I am *not* stupid."

"I'm sure you are not, Giorgio, and people can be very cruel sometimes."

"Yes," he agreed, "they can. Can I get you anything else?"

"The bathroom, perhaps?"

"Certainly. We will go down the hall, but I must wait for you — outside, just as before."

"Of course," Donna said. She was, after all, still his prisoner.

Chapter 18

While the Vitellis and Iams were still at breakfast, Police Lieutenant Matteo Giudice was already in conference with his boss, Captain Carlo Benedetto, head of the St. Mark's Square station. Were it not for the fancy uniform, Benedetto was almost a doppelganger for Captain Parker, Vitelli's American boss: short and round, with a fleshy face. He also shared Parker's somewhat ornery and suspicious disposition.

"We have had plenty of tourists disappear before — almost always they turn up eventually. But never in my experience was there an actual kidnapping. You are sure this man, *Signore* Iams, is reliable, and his wife did not just take off on him, Giudice?"

"I am, Captain — especially since the American policeman, Detective Vitelli, confirmed his story."

Benedetto grunted. "That is another thing. The American policeman, this Vitelli, I am not so sure you are right about him. And that is an Italian name, no? And this Vitelli speaks no Italian? Why is that, do you think?"

"You would have to ask him, Captain. But I would guess he was born over there, and, in America, everyone speaks English."

"A guttural tongue. But, unlike you, I have never been to America. New York, was it?"

"No, Captain. Chicago. And then only for two weeks."

"And that was enough for you to learn English, eh?"

"No, Captain. I studied English at university."

"Ah. I forget. You are an educated man."

Benedetto had never said as much, but Giudice had long ago gotten the distinct impression that his boss resented his university education, and subsequent rapid rise through the ranks. It had taken Benedetto ten years to make sergeant, another four to become a lieutenant. He did finally make captain, but only after accumulating some twenty-two years on the force. In contrast, Giudice had been recruited out of university, graduated from Police Academy as a sergeant, and had made lieutenant in just two years.

"This Vitelli," he continued, "the American policeman. You asked him for his assistance on this case? That was a foolish move. Why ever would you do that, Lieutenant?"

Unfazed, Giudice said, "Two reasons, Captain. First, *Signore* Iams trusts him, and appears to defer to him where the abduction of his wife is concerned. It was Vitelli, after all, who convinced him to ignore the kidnappers' instructions and come to the police for help in the first place. And second, whereas, and as you have just said, we have had practically no experience with an actual kidnapping, this *Signore* Vitelli has."

"Yes. In America. The Wild West. Cowboys and Indians. But we don't operate that way in Italy, and that is a good thing." He paused, as if in reflection. "Well, I suppose what is done is done. Just make sure this Vitelli character does not get under foot, and do not tell him anything he does not need to know. Now, I know we are waiting for the kidnappers to contact Iams with their demands. What have you done in the meantime?"

"I put the word out on the street immediately, asking if any one of our confidential informants has heard anything."

"Good. And?"

"Word this morning—from Cherino Gubbio, who lives up by the Misericordia Abby, in the east end of the Cannaregio section of the city. He was walking his dog along the canal there late yesterday morning, and saw two men rushing a small, chubby, elderly woman out of a boat and onto the quay. They were rushing her along and then disappeared up one of the alleyways. He did not see where they went."

"And why might that be significant?"

"Because Gubbio knows these two men, describes them as lowlifes like himself. And the old woman was wearing a blue pants suit, as was Donna Iams when last her husband and the Vitellis saw her at breakfast that morning."

"So, *if* this was the same woman, then she is still in Venice. Gubbio, does he have names for the two men he saw?"

"Not names, exactly. Street names. One, a big man, is called Hulk. The other, small and thin, is called Serb. He gave us descriptions of each, but they are pretty vague. They may or may not be in out mugshot library.

Certainly, there are no photos of men there associated with those street names."

"Very well. But we are looking for them, of course?"

"We are, sir, and I have notified *Comandante* Rubio at our command station there, and they are looking for them as well."

Benedetto looked annoyed. "I doubt that that was really necessary. You should not have bothered the commander. This case is in our jurisdiction, after all. But what is done is done. For now, how about we sit and wait for the kidnappers to make their move?"

"Yes, sir. Now we sit and wait."

Chapter 19

Giudice was still at his desk when Vitelli showed up at the station, Pam in tow. Apparently, the beautiful Sergeant Capello was not on duty that day. That day's desk clerk, a uniformed young man, was asking in Italian who they were, and what their business with the police was, when Giudice spied them and hurried over.

"Never mind, Sergeant, I know this gentleman and his wife," Giudice said in Italian. Switching to English, he said, "Detective Vitelli, *Signora*, what brings you here? Have the what-do-you-call, 'kidnappers,' have they contacted Iams?"

"Not exactly, Lieutenant, but almost." He then told him about the cell phone and its accompanying instructions that Iams had received that morning. Pam stayed silent, but missed nothing.

"Very clever of them. He cannot identify people he has never seen. *Signora* Iams can confirm that she is well over the telephone, and these kidnappers never have to show themselves. It might be helpful if we had that instruction note."

"I thought you might want it. Here it is," and Vitelli drew a slip of paper encased in a plastic envelope and handed it over to Giudice. "Probably useless for fingerprints. I'm afraid it had already been handled by Calvin Iams, myself, and the desk clerk at the hotel."

"Of course," Giudice said, taking it, "but, still, you have done well to bag it as soon as you could. But, then, you know that. Now let me tell you what we have found out."

Despite Captain Benedetto's instructions to the contrary, Giudice filled Vitelli in on Cherino Gubbio's report. "It fits," Vitelli said. "The timing is about right, and the woman does fit Donna's description. At least it's an indication that she's being held in the city."

"Yes. So now we sit and wait."

"We sit and wait. Say, when they call, is there any way we can tell where they are calling from?"

"Not really. The operating cell towers vary with the what-do-you-call — the 'corporation? — the one that operates the cell phones?"

"The carrier," Vitelli suggested.

"Yes. The carrier. And there are four carriers that serve the city. We would need to identify the particular cell towers that served that particular call, before we could determine where the call originated. And we could only do that, if they stayed on the line long enough. So, such a thing is beyond us, I am afraid."

"I see."

"I know. They do these things on the TV all the time," Giudice apologized, "but unfortunately, reality has not caught up with the TV."

Chapter 20

"We have to get back to the hotel and tell Cal what the lieutenant told us. He'll want to know that Donna's probably still in the city," Vitelli said,

"Cal will be in meetings this morning, remember?" Pam replied. "You *did* tell him to behave as if nothing had happened. Now how about we do somewhat that same thing! We're in Venice! On our honeymoon! Why don't you to take me on a gondola ride? It'll only take about an hour, and we can go see Cal after that."

THEY FOUND DOZENS OF gondolas tied up off the quay at St. Mark's.

"Pick one," Vitelli said.

"But they're all the same. And all painted black. Why is that, I wonder?"

A handsome young man in a blue and white, horizontally striped shirt and a straw hat had suddenly appeared beside them. "It's the law," he said in a pleasantly accented English. "Since the sixteenth century. All gondolas are *required* to be painted black."

"Really?" Pam said.

"Really," he said. "I am Antonio. Would you like me to be your gondolier?"

"How much for a ride?" Vitelli asked.

"Much more than it's worth, perhaps. One hundred euros," Antonio said with a smile. "But the *Signore* looks like he can afford it! Besides, you cannot leave Venice without riding in a gondola! Come, *Signore, Signora,* your gondola awaits!" He directed them to one in a group of a dozen-or-so boats tied up alongside the quay.

"Be careful getting in," Antonio warned, as he took Pam by the hand and sat her on one side of the tiny cabin. He then held out his hand, and once Rich gave him two fifty-euro notes, he pointed to the place next to Pam. "And you, *Signore,* sit please over here." When they were both settled, he said, "You will note that the boat is wider on one side than the other. That is so it is in balance when I stand in the back, and to one side, to drive it. But that different wideness and the flat bottom, they also make the gondola a little bit unstable if you move around too much, eh?"

With that, he untied the boat from the quay, and, standing in the stern, and using just a single oar on one side of the boat, sculled it out expertly out into the Grand Canal. But they were not in the Grand Canal for long, as Antonio quickly guided the boat into the canal directly behind the Doge's Palace. "This is the *Rio di Palazzo,*" Antonio announced. "To the left is the rear of the Doge's Palace, to the right, the prison.

"On one's honeymoon," he continued, "you, *Signore,* must kiss the bride as we pass under the Bridge of Sighs. It is tradition!"

"Wait," Vitelli said, "how did you know we were on our honeymoon?"

"Ah, *Signore,*" he said, "Antonio can feel the love!" With that he broke out into song, and Rich dutifully kissed Pam as they passed under the Bridge of Sighs.

The hour passed quickly, as Antonio snaked the boat through some other connecting canals, ducking under narrow bridges, regaled Pam and Rich with local fables and pointed out the sights as they passed. When he wasn't talking, he was singing.

"The songs you sing are beautiful, Antonio," Pam said. "Are they Venetian songs?"

"Oh no, *Signora,* they are Neapolitan songs, not Venetian."

"Why Neapolitan songs, Antonio, and not Venetian?"

"Because, *Signora,*" Antonio said with a wink, "the Venetians are the merchants, but the Neapolitans, they are the lovers!"

Before they knew it, they were back in the Grand Canal, the gondola emerging just upstream of the Rialto Bridge. There, Antonio turned the boat left and guided it under the bridge. He drove the boat another short distance, and then they entered another side canal to the left. "The *Rio di San Luca*" Antonio announced. Then there were more fables, more low bridges for Antonio to duck under, more local sights, more serenading.

Once more, the gondola emerged onto the Grand Canal, just opposite the magnificent *Santa Maria Salute* church on the tip of the *Punta della Dogana.* Antonio again turned left, and soon the Vitellis were back where they had started, at the quay next to St. Marks. Somehow, the hour had passed, and Antonio was helping them out of the boat and onto the quay.

"I just loved that," Pam sighed, as they started walking back toward the Accademia.

Chapter 21

Anubis Cline sat in the beautifully-furnished lounge aboard the borrowed yacht in the Italian port of Trieste, just fifty nautical miles east-northeast across the Adriatic from Venice. Cline had cashed in on an old debt, and had the hundred-meter craft and its crew for the entire month, *gratis*. Just the type of arrangement that suited the frugal Cline the best.

Securely fastened to a wall shelf not far from where Cline's bulk was relaxing on a tan leather settee, was the solid gold urn that held the ashes of his late lamented ward, Jael—blind, beautiful, exotic, Jael, who gave her life that Cline might retain his.

That event had taken place the better part of two years earlier, when, back home in the city, a woman named Charlene Morton had broken into Cline's West Lakeside home. Morton, had been the close associate of the murdered billionaire Sheldon Hertz, one of Cline's clients. Morton had determined that it was Cline who had arranged Hertz's death, and she was bent on killing him in turn.

Knife in hand, she had attacked Cline in his bed. As fate would have it, however, she was well into accomplishing her goal, when Cline's beloved ward, Jael, attacked Morton, pulling her off Cline. Morton, striking back at Jael, then stabbed her fatally.

Cline, now given the time to retrieve a pistol from his bedstand, shot Morton, killing her in turn. The police investigation concluded that Cline had acted in self-defense.

Now, all Cline had left of the only person in the world he ever loved, was a gold urn containing her ashes.

He was lost in thought, gazing at her remains, when his satellite telephone rang.

Calling was Cline's connection in Venice. "Well, Charlie," asked Cline, "how is our little enterprise progressing?"

"According to plan, Reaper. *Signore* Iams is scared witless. As long as we are holding his wife, I am sure he will cooperate, and do exactly as we wish."

"That is the plan. But then Iams has only a small role to play—merely to see to it that the artwork is loaded aboard our boat safely on Sunday night. I assume he disobeyed his instructions and has contacted the police?"

"He has. And the *Tenente* Giudice assigned to the case is green, and should pose no problem. There is one new development, however. Iams has a friend here in Venice, a detective from America, one familiar with kidnapping cases. Giudice has asked for his assistance and has agreed to keep him informed. He's an American policeman named Vitelli—Richard Vitelli."

Cline's jaw dropped. "Vitelli, you say? Richard Vitelli?" *What? Here in Italy?*" (Vitelli was one of the police officers who had investigated Jael's murder, and who had cost Cline a great deal of money in the Bobby Doyle kidnapping affair.) "And what exactly, Charlie, is this Vitelli person doing there in Venice?"

"As I understand it, Reaper, he and his new wife are here on their honeymoon."

It figures, Cline mused. *God, if there is one, has a remarkable sense of humor! But no matter. We have dealt with Detective Lieutenant Richard Vitelli in the past, and outmaneuvered him, and we will do so again, now.* "No matter, Charlie. Here in Italy, Vitelli is a duck out of water—no acquaintance with the territory, and no authority whatever. Pay attention, rather, to your local Lieutenant Giudice. He could well gum up the works."

"Believe me, Reaper, I will continue to keep a close eye on him. He *has* managed to locate an informant who saw my two men—the ones charged with abducting and keeping the Iams woman quiet—hustling her along on one of the docks in the Cannaregio. So, they have an idea that the woman is still in Venice, but they cannot be sure. And, even if they were sure, they know only approximately where in the city she is—a complication, perhaps, but certainly not a fatal one."

"See to it that it isn't," Cline said. "And about those two men, the Iams woman can now identify them. That might become a problem for you eventually. Perhaps they, or the woman, should be dealt with once their usefulness to us is over. You need to think about that, Charlie."

"I will, *Signore.*"

"Good. You have little enough to do, Charlie, and you are being handsomely rewarded for your part in our little enterprise. I leave it up to you to handle these little details."

"Yes, Reaper, I will see to it," a somewhat defiant Charlie replied. *You may well be the master planner, Reaper, Charlie thought, and you may pay very well, but it is me, and my little band, who will have to actually steal the paintings, and take all the risks!*

Chapter 22

Calvin Iams was still in the meeting with the Oppenheim's director and his staff; they were planning the taking down of the American exhibit, and the re-crating of the artwork for its transport back to the States. The special phone in his left jacket pocket rang. His personal cell phone was in his right jacket pocket.

"Excuse me," he said, "I have to take this." He quickly rose from his chair and left the room, oblivious the disapproving glares from museum director Grimaldi and his staff.

He didn't answer the phone until he was outside the museum. "Hello?" he finally said.

"Took you long enough."

Iams recognized the accent of the man that had first contacted him. "I was in a meeting. I couldn't very well answer the phone in front of the others."

"When we call, you answer, and quick," Serb said.

"I *did* answer. And as quickly as I could," Iams replied, apologetically.

"You do not appear to realize how serious we are, *Signore* Iams. We told you not to contact the police, but you did anyway, didn't you?"

There were a few seconds of silence on the line, as Iams, tongue-tied, was unable to say anything. Serb snickered, and continued. "Did you forget we have your wife?" He paused for effect. "But, okay. Here is what you must do—"

"I will do nothing, not until I know my wife is safe and well!" Iams interrupted.

"I thought you might say that. Okay. Here. Speak, woman!"

"Cal?"

"Donna? Is that you? Are you okay?"

"Yes, Cal, it's me. I'm scared Cal. They haven't hurt me, but they're keeping me—"

"That is enough," Serb's voice broke in. "So now you know, Iams, your wife is okay. But it is up to you to be sure she stays that way."

"I understand," Iams replied.

"Good. Now here is what you must do. But first, you are taking the paintings down this coming Sunday, no?"

"Yes, after the museum closes on Sunday—that evening. Then we will ready them for shipment by putting them in their individual crates. All twelve of them."

"Good. And what time is the boat for them due at the museum dock?"

"Early Monday morning—one o'clock. But there will be a security escort on the powered lighter. It's a shallow-draft boat that's coming for them."

"I know what a lighter is. And I know about the security escort. This is what you must do. Simply see to it that the paintings are safely stowed on whatever vessel *does* come for them. *Securely* stowed. Understand?"

"*Securely* stowed. I understand."

"And no messing about. The real paintings are to be in those crates. If you try to switch them with others, we will know, and your wife will die."

"You have made that very clear. Now, will you let me talk to my wife again?"

"Maybe next time," Serb said, and the phone went dead.

Chapter 23

On the whole, despite the comforts the yacht provided, Anubis Cline — Reaper — decided he would much rather be home, back in the city, in his modest mansion overlooking the lake.

When his murdered ward, Jael, was alive, he would frequently discuss situations and opportunities with her. Jael would be a sounding board for his various schemes and plots. Her value lay in what was, in his mind, her complete objectivity; like him, she completely lacked the ability to shrink away from pursuing the most expeditious course of action, no matter how illegal or immoral. The end always justified the means.

It had taken an entire year for Cline to fight off a profound depression and come to terms with the loss of his beloved ward, Jael. But he finally had — in his own peculiar way. His recourse, finally, was simply to resurrect her in his mind, whenever the occasion called for it, and engage her in an imaginary conversation. He was, in a way, praying to her as one might pray to a saint, and was able to hear her responses in his head.

ANUBIS CLINE ONCE AGAIN retreated back into a world of his own making. He conjured up a vision of his ward, Jael, and saw her so clearly, he could almost reach out and touch her — even though her only real physical presence was the urn containing her ashes, fixed to the shelf above his head.

Jael, my child, I miss our home. There I had my control center, my base of operations. I felt so much more in control than I do in this moving bathtub!

"I understand, Abba," she replied in his mind's eye, "*but you are here now, and this promises to be a most lucrative adventure. Stay the course. Soon, you will have a new and magnificent piece of artwork in your personal collection, and the remaining eleven pieces will each bring in a small fortune. You already have the buyers lined up, and we stand to make millions!*"

But I worry, child. These Italians are not as reliable and predictable as the people I work with back home. There are many elements to this enterprise and they must all mesh together perfectly. And Charlie. Compared to the Russian, Korborov, who I employed for our last venture, Charlie is an amateur. And of all people to show up out of the blue — Vitelli! Even in his ignorance, the man has a habit of costing me money. He is bad karma.

"Be that as it may, Abba, but remember you have bested Vitelli in the past, and now you will do so again. And as for Charlie, that is who you must work with. Charlie is best placed to assure that this operation comes to a successful conclusion. This is the time, and Venice is the place. Outside of a major museum, nowhere else in the world are twelve such valuable paintings assembled in one place, and in such a vulnerable situation. Only during their transport will they be so available, so ripe for the picking. You can do this!"

Ah, child, I revel in your confidence. Of course, you are right. We will prevail. But I would be so much more comfortable in my cozy office back home, that is all.

IT HAD COME TO Cline months ago, while he was perusing the hometown newspaper.

No longer provided in print, the city's newspaper was now published only in an electronic format, available for a modest subscription fee. Cline used to enjoy reading the physical newspaper from front to back every morning after breakfast. He could sit back in his easy chair and read at his ease. Now he had to sit in his office chair and read from a computer screen. *This was progress?* he thought.

There was this article about how the Metro Foundation Museum of Art was arranging an art exhibit for the Arts Festival Week in Venice, Italy. Twelve modern art masterpieces, gathered from museums across America, were to be shipped to the Museum of Modern Art in New York for consolidation and transshipment to Venice. The exhibition would be hosted in Venice by the Linda Oppenheim Museum. The article noted that the Metro Foundation Museum's director, Calvin Iams, would be traveling to Venice to serve as the exhibition's curator.

The article went on to credit Iams' brilliant young assistant, Pamela Karns, with setting up the show, and then went on to list the contributing American museums and which artworks they were lending. But, by then, Anubis Cline had already been formulating in his mind how he might go about using the event to steal the paintings and make millions.

It had been easy enough to set the gears in motion. Simply put a call out on the dark web, on just the right websites, for a willing partner in Venice, Italy. There were, surprisingly, several replies. The person selected was ideally connected for the scheme, someone who was well acquainted with, and could recruit from, the Venetian underworld, someone also in a unique position to monitor whatever action the local authorities might take to thwart the venture. Cline had found "Charlie," and Charlie had found "Reaper," as Cline had chosen to call himself online.

Chapter 24

As soon as Iams had told him about the phone call he had received, Vitelli made a reticent Calvin Iams contact Lieutenant Giudice and give him the details. The Vitellis were with him as he called Giudice from his hotel room. Iams put the call on speakerphone, so the Rich and Pam could listen in.

After Iams filled him in on the contents of the kidnapper's call, Giudice's first question was, "Your wife, she sounded okay?"

"She did. Scared, maybe, but okay."

"Very well. And the person on the phone told you not to try and switch the paintings, and to be sure that they were secure on the vessel that arrived to pick them up?"

"He did."

"You are sure? He wanted you to make sure the paintings were securely, what-do-you-call-it, 'stowed?'"

"Yes. Securely stowed. I can only assume to ensure they cannot shift in transit. He was very emphatic about that."

"Now I am worried. Tell me, Mister Iams, what were the arrangements for this lighter and the transportation of the paintings?"

"The powered lighter and its crew are coming out from the port, set to arrive at the Accademia dock at midnight, Sunday night. The crew will load the paintings aboard her—twelve crates, each with a painting—and then transport them north of the city to the Marco Polo Airport. A cargo plane will be waiting there to fly them to New York, via London Heathrow."

"So, the lighter would never have to leave the lagoon," Giudice said. "But they could possibly intend to replace the lighter with another vessel. And, again, you were to be sure the paintings were securely—stowed?"

"That's what they said."

Vitelli broke in. "What are you thinking, Matteo?"

"Well, if the paintings were to be transported according to the route *Signore* Iams just described, then, the powered lighter, with its flat bottom, built for navigation in shallow, protected, waters, would be the perfect transport. It never needs to leave the lagoon. So, to secure the paintings would not be all that critical. But, if they were planning to take a different route, say, out into the Adriatic, the waters there are not so calm, and to secure the paintings would be *very* critical. And *then*, the boat the crooks would send to pick up the paintings would have to be one designed to go out to sea."

"Makes sense," Vitelli said. "So, what do we do next?"

"Next, I report to my Captain. He insists that he and I meet at least daily, and that I update him on every bit of progress made, and on every new bit of information learned. I will update him of this latest news." Giudice paused for a breath, as if gathering his thoughts, and continued. "But I shall urge Captain Benedetto to now direct two things — first, that our men be on that lighter. It is possible that the thieves have a plan to invade it, take it over, and replace the crew with their own men. They might do this before, or after, the lighter is used to pick up the paintings. They will have another way to get the paintings out of the lagoon, if necessary, perhaps even by using their own aircraft. We will want to be on that lighter to prevent that plan from ever getting, how-do-you-say, 'off the ground?'

"But alternatively, they may plan to ambush the lighter, discard it, and replace it with a deep-water vessel, a vessel capable of sailing out of the lagoon and going out to sea. So, secondly then, we should also have our men by the Accademia dock, so that whatever vessel arrives to pick up the paintings, we can stop them from stealing the paintings, and arrest the men on board."

"Sounds about right," Vitelli agreed. "Which do you think is the most likely scenario?"

"Well," Giudice said, "the first one, taking over the lighter, and using it to transport the artwork, is simpler. But the second, using another boat altogether, would not confine them to the lagoon. Their overall plan may make it necessary for them to go out into the Adriatic. They did, after all, direct *Signore* Iams to ensure the paintings were secure."

"Whatever they're planning," Vitelli agreed, "you're right. We need to have your men both on the lighter, and at the museum."

Gene Masters

Chapter 25

Anchored to the floor of the Adriatic Sea, ten miles southeast of Venice, stands a monitoring tower. The sole purpose of the tower is to monitor the sea level and measure climate conditions: wind strength and direction, and atmospheric pressure. The tower is replete with the instruments that record the vital data, and computers that run the models that interpret those data.

The sea level will normally vary, and three things will affect it: tide, wind, and atmospheric pressure.

First of all, the sea level will vary with the tide. The height of the tide is measured over time and graphed on a computer. That data will generate a sine wave — a line with troughs and crests looking very much like an undulating snake, or a dragon. The message: the tides vary. They vary in height and across time because of the Earth's rotation and the gravitational pull of the Sun and the Moon.

Over the entire Earth, the tide varies daily with the rotation of the Earth; every day has its high tide and its low tide. The range of tides also vary monthly; depending on the time of the month, the measured high tide will be much higher than low tide, or, at other times, not so high.

When the Earth and the Moon are in line with the Sun, the difference between high and low tide is the greatest. This happens twice a month, every month, and this is the time the daily high tides are at their highest: the *spring* tide. Also, twice a month, every month, when the Sun and the Moon are at right angles to each other, the daily high tides will be at their lowest levels: the *neap* tide.

Second, especially in the Adriatic, tides can vary with wind direction:

The Adriatic is a relatively narrow body of water open to the Mediterranean on the South, and closed off by land in the north. The prevailing wind plays a big part in determining water depth. When the wind is flowing from north to south, Adriatic waters will be pushed into the Mediterranean, and the Adriatic empties. Water levels will decrease overall. When the opposite happens, and the wind blows up from the Mediterranean, pushing its water up into the Adriatic, then water levels in the Adriatic will increase.

Exactly how much the wind affects the water level in the Adriatic obviously depends on the strength of the wind. Occasionally, a *very* strong wind, called a *Scirocco*, blows up from the Mediterranean, and the water level in the Adriatic rises dramatically and significantly.

Finally, atmospheric pressure plays a part.

When the pressure is high, the weight of the air presses down on the water, tending to level it, and lowers the overall seawater level. The opposite occurs with low atmospheric pressure, and overall sea level is higher.

Combine a spring tide, a strong wind blowing up from the south, and a low-pressure trough, and conditions in the Adriatic are perfect for *Acqua Alta* in Venice: the so-called *surge* tide.

And that is why the monitoring tower sits in the Adriatic ten miles from the city, to provide for adequate warning to the residents of the danger of flooding, and to allow the engineers adequate time to employ MOSE [MOSE stands for *Modulo Sperimentale Elettromeccanico* in Italian, or the Experimental Electromechanical Module] and mitigate the flooding.

Genaro Delmonico is one of the engineers tasked to visit the monitoring tower and evaluate the sea conditions on a regular basis. The trip from the city takes just over an hour by boat, and Genaro makes the trip at least every other day — more often if sea conditions warrant. Today, Genaro is making the trip for the second day in a row.

Yesterday, the conditions recorded at the tower, coupled with the weather reports from stations in the Mediterranean, were cause for concern. He had run the computer models, but the model results were inconclusive. He suspected that today's results might be quite different.

Today, once on the tower, he followed his usual routine: reading the recorded data, pairing them with the reports from the stations in the south, and entering them into the computer, and then running the simulation models. Today the models were all in agreement. There would be a surge tide, and it would be at its highest level at 0323 next Monday morning, or three hours, twenty-three minutes after Sunday midnight. Genaro got on the radio and conveyed his findings to the MOSE control center in the city.

The MOSE control center in Venice, is in the *Arsenale*, or Arsenal section of the city, just to the northeast of St. Marks. It was in the Arsenal where the Venetian ships were once built, the ships that ruled the seas in the city's maritime heyday. Today, in the control center, Genaro's boss, Justino Carrillo, began preparations to deploy the MOSE. He would check Genaro's calculations, of course, and rerun the simulations on the computers in the control center, but that was just quality assurance; it was almost certain that Genaro had interpreted the data correctly. *Acqua Alta* was coming, and it was coming in the wee hours of next Monday morning.

Chapter 26

"You have done well, Giudice," Captain Benedetto said. "And, of course, we will station our men both aboard the lighter and at the Accademia dock."

Matteo Giudice smiled. He had not thought that Benedetto would agree so easily to his proposed plans.

"Our first job will be to make sure these thieves do not waylay the lighter," Benedetto continued, "and that it, and it alone, will be the vessel used to transport the paintings to the airport—and the airport that receives them must be Marco Polo.

"But then we must also intercept any replacement vessel, if, in fact, there is a replacement vessel. To do that, we must have a force at the museum to capture its crew and then find out where they had planned to take the paintings. We may then be able to find out who planned this operation, and perhaps even break up the crime ring behind it."

"That would be good, Captain," Giudice said, inasmuch as his captain had just directed the implementation of the action plan he had proposed just minutes before.

"I will see to it that there are men stationed at the museum, Lieutenant. But I want you to be on that lighter, and to ultimately ensure that those paintings get safely to the airport. You will have sufficient men aboard, of course, to thwart any attempt to take over the vessel on its way to the museum."

"Yes, Captain," Giudice acknowledged. He would rather have been in command of the museum contingent, actually making sure that the paintings remained safe, but that was not his call. Benedetto was the boss. He thought again about his conversation with Vitelli, that there was the greater possibility that the thieves would be using a second boat. If so, being on the lighter meant very likely being away from the action. He was unhappy about that. But again, Benedetto was the boss,

"I will be glad when that so-called artwork is aboard that plane and is on its way safely out of Venice," Benedetto continued. "Once those paintings are gone from the city, they will no longer be our responsibility, and only then can I breathe easy."

For once, Giudice and his captain were in total agreement.

Chapter 27

Whether it was a conscious decision or not, the Vitellis avoided Calvin Iams over the next two days that remained for the American exhibition at the Oppenheim. When they did see him, it was obvious that the man was mentally operating on automatic, going through the motions until the following Sunday night, when he would either cooperate with the looting of millions of dollars' worth of fine art, or the love of his life would surely be murdered. Then, of course, there was also the nagging reality that she might be murdered anyway, even if he *did* cooperate.

They took advantage of the time to do some of what they came to Venice to do in the first place: act as average tourists. They took the ferry to Murano on Friday morning, and watched the Venetian glass blowers ply their art. With an eye to buying just what they could easily transport back to the States, Pam bought only several small glass trinkets: glass blown to resemble pieces of fruit, tiny bows, and little animals.

They then took the ferry back to Venice, planning on having a late lunch in the trattoria they discovered on their first night in the city.

Pam and Rich had selected the items that filled their plates, and were on their way to find a place to sit, when they spied Lieutenant Giudice, accompanied by the lovely Sergeant Capello. Both were in street clothes and obviously off duty. Giudice wore tan slacks and an open shirt; Capello was in a breezy yellow linen dress.

"Matteo!" Vitelli called out, getting the lieutenant's attention. Giudice, hearing his name, looked around for the source of the hailing, and recognized Rich and Pam. Vitelli thought that Matteo's first look was one of guilt, immediately followed by one of relief, when he recognized who it was that had hailed him.

"Rich," Giudice said, as he and the sergeant approached, "how nice to see you and Pam! You both know Carlotta from the office, no?" Then to Sergeant Capello: "Carlotta, you remember Rich and Pam Vitelli?"

"Of course," Carlotta Capello said. "How nice to see you again—thankfully, of course, under more pleasant circumstances. How is poor *Signore* Iams holding up?" Vitelli noted that her command of English had somehow improved since their first meeting.

"As well as can be expected under the circumstances, I'm afraid."

"Then we must pray that all will be made right at the end, no?" Carlotta said.

"Exactly," Pam agreed. "But surely you must both join us for lunch?"

"That will be our pleasure. Right, Matteo?" Carlotta said, looking up at him.

"Of course," Giudice agreed, though a little reluctantly, or at least so it seemed to Vitelli. "Please—you go ahead and find a place for the four of us to sit, while Carlotta and I get our meals."

Which they did. Soon, they joined the Vitellis. They spent a pleasant meal together, mostly talking small talk, each one learning something about each other, becoming friends. The Vitellis learned that the *carabinieri* discouraged fraternization among the ranks, and the couple swore them to secrecy. The Vitellis readily agreed.

After they had parted, Rich remarked to Pam that Matteo and Carlotta made a handsome couple. Pam replied, "Yes, they do. But I think that Matteo is far more interested in Carlotta than she is with him.

"Why do you say that?" Vitelli asked.

"I don't know," Pam replied, "just a feeling."

That evening there was a concert in St. Mark's Square. The orchestra played an all-Italian selection: Italian folk tunes, operatic selections from Verdi and Puccini, and some Vivaldi.

Chapter 28

Saturday was spent with Pam and Rich further exploring the city, but only after Vitelli met with Giudice at the station that morning with a suggestion.

First Giudice gave Vitelli a quick rundown on the plans for Sunday night and Monday morning. Then Vitelli offered, "When I was in the Navy, our life jackets had little salt-water-activated radio transmitters attached to them. They put out a constant radio signal that our ships could use to locate, and pick up, a man in the water. Something much simpler could be attached to one of the shipping crates containing the artwork. You know, a device that could put out a radio signal that could be tracked by a patrol boat or an aircraft."

"But why would such a device be required, if the thieves are not allowed to get anywhere near the artwork to begin with?" Giudice asked.

"It wouldn't. But we must not automatically assume success. What if, in the end, we aren't able to foil their attempts to get anywhere near the paintings? We must always consider the possibility that things will go terribly wrong, that the artwork will be stolen, and plan for its recovery as well."

"You mean provide for the possibility that they *will* manage to steal the paintings?"

"Exactly."

"And if they do manage," Giudice acknowledged, "then the transmitter would give us a way to at least locate them."

"Yes."

"Makes sense. Very good sense. I will pass the idea on to the captain. I am sure, though, that he will approve it."

"Good, but let's just hope we'll never need it. I'm disappointed that your captain decided to put you on the lighter. I'd rather you were in charge of the contingent at dockside."

"It was not my decision," Giudice said. Vitelli caught the trace of disappointment in his voice.

Once again, Giudice was surprised when his captain quickly agreed with the plan to attach a radio transmitter in among the crates containing the paintings. But now he was tasked with finding one, since the station had no such device in its inventory.

Chapter 29

That Sunday, at breakfast, a worn-out-looking Calvin Iams joined the Vitellis at breakfast.

"You look beat," Rich observed. "Are you getting any sleep at all?"

"Not much," Iams admitted. "I've been up the past couple of nights late, anyway. Working, setting up, getting the paintings ready for shipment as soon as the exhibition is over."

"Have you heard anything more about Donna?" Pam asked.

"The bastards called me around noon yesterday. Warned me again that I was to cooperate fully with their people, or they would kill her. Then they put her on the phone for just a few seconds—she said she was okay, and wasn't being treated badly. I'm sure they did that—let her talk to me—just to prove that she was still alive."

"And you didn't let Giudice know this?" Vitelli scolded.

"What's the point?" Iams replied wearily. "It was hardly new or pertinent information."

"Perhaps not. And all this comes to a head at midnight tonight," Vitelli said.

"I guess," was Iams wan reply. "But there's still some stuff I need to do between now and then. So, as soon as we're finished here, I'm back to the Oppenheim."

LATER THAT SAME SUNDAY morning, the Vitellis attended the eleven o'clock Mass at St. Marks Basilica. It was the last day of the Arts Festival, and inside the Basilica, seated on either side of the sanctuary, was a full orchestra and chorus.

Vitelli was once again blown away by the basilica to begin with, with its 800-year-old, soaring dome and arches, its interior all wrought in pure gold, and covered with beautiful mosaics — biblical themes, sacred symbols, images of angels and saints.

The Mass was a long one, sung in Latin and Italian by the chorus, with the chorus accompanied by the orchestra. The *Gloria* alone took a full ten minutes to sing, not that anyone was timing it. The biblical readings and homily were delivered, of course, in Italian.

Pam and Rich, as well as everyone else in attendance, were carried away by the sheer beauty of the music and the solemnity of the ceremony. After the Communion, and the final "*Ite, Missa est*" sending, the celebrants and attendants filed out of the sanctuary. Pam and Rich assumed it was time to leave, but nobody was leaving their seats. It was then that the orchestra and chorus broke into the Hallelujah chorus from Handel's *Messiah*. Only when the music stopped, and the last note had been sung, did anyone in the basilica make a move to reluctantly get up, and leave the church.

"My God, Rich," Pam said on leaving, "That was just so beautiful!"

They had a late breakfast at one of the bistros lining St. Mark's square. It was expensive, but for Vitelli, the location was convenient. "Wait here," he said to a puzzled-looking Pam, "I'll be right back." She assumed he was leaving to find a men's room, and just smiled her assent. But Vitelli had something else in mind.

"AND WHAT IS THE range on that thing?" Vitelli asked Giudice. He had met the Italian Lieutenant in his office, just across the square where he and Pam had just finished breakfast.

"Four or five kilometers, more or less. It sends out a continuous signal on the emergency band, 156.050 MHz, and the battery is supposed to last for days."

"Sounds good. Amazing, though. That thing is so tiny."

"Have Iams put it in with one of the paintings. Let us hope it is, what-do-you-call, 'overkill,' eh?"

"Understood. But I'm not going to have Iams do it. The less he knows about any backup plan, the better. I'll figure out a way to get the transmitter in with one of the paintings myself."

"Okay. Perhaps you are right, and it is best *Signore* Iams be kept in the dark about the transmitter. Give him at least one less thing to worry about. But you must not fail to plant it among the paintings, and, for the sake of heaven, do not forget to turn it on, eh?"

"Okay. I won't," Vitelli chuckled. "Now I have to get back to my wife. She's waiting for me in the square, and she'll be wondering what I've been up to!"

Chapter 30

Sunday evening came, and Rich splurged on a sit-down dinner in one of the city's better restaurants, Lineadombra, not far from their hotel. Dining was on the water — literally — on a floating terrace anchored to the north bank of the Giudecca Canal. The house specialty was seafood, and as an appetizer, the Vitellis ate their fill of fresh mussels, cooked in a spicy broth. Pam followed them with something called *luccio alla gardesana,* a poached fish served on a bed of fresh vegetables and fried polenta. Rich eschewed any more seafood, and elected instead for the *Bistecca alla Milanese.* A dry white *Cervero della Sala* wine went well with dinner, although the waiter rolled his eyes when he saw Rich drink the white wine with his beef. There was no room for dessert, and espresso was finally served, complete with a curl of lemon peel for each cup.

A stroll back to the hotel rounded out the evening.

"When we get back to the hotel, you're not coming up to the room, are you," Pam said, a statement, not a question.

"No," Rich replied. "You know I can't. The paintings are due to be shipped from the museum tonight. I need to be there, be sure that they get shipped out safely."

"But haven't you done enough? You have no authority here, you know that. Let Lieutenant Giudice and his crew handle it. It's their job, after all, not yours."

"I know that. But Cal and Donna are our friends, and Cal needs me there for moral support, if for nothing else." *Besides, I need to plant a transmitter in with the paintings.*

Pam shuddered. "I guess I understand. But it's not Cal I'm worried about so much as Donna. It's not knowing if she's alive or dead."

"Well, we know she was alive as of yesterday noon, when Cal spoke to her."

"We can only pray she stays that way."

"That's about all we really can do. No telling what those people will do once they have what they want."

Pam shuddered again.

Chapter 31

It was a little after ten o'clock when Vitelli knocked at the back door of the museum. The meager lighting outside the museum fought a losing battle against the darkness of the night. The Venetian weather had been mild until then, but it had turned cloudy earlier, and now it had become damp and chilly, the sky black, threatening rain. A waning moon peeped out only occasionally, and even then, it was low in the sky, providing little added light.

Iams opened the door and ushered Vitelli into what was a workroom and storage facility at the rear, *Fondamenta Venier* entrance. Inside were work tables, cabinets, and tool chests. Two walls were lined with deep racks, paintings stacked upright against them, separated by protective foam core boards. In the center of the room were twelve narrow crates.

"I assume those are the paintings, ready for shipment," Vitelli said.

"They are," Iams said. "Lieutenant Giudice was by earlier. Said he had a boat waiting to take him and his men to the lighter. He said his mission was to make sure it made it here on time and without incident."

"Good. He left some people behind, I hope? Make sure everything stays quiet on this end?"

"No, he didn't. Said his captain would be sending some men over later to guard the paintings, and to intercept the other boat, if there is one. He thought there shouldn't be a problem. He also advised that our own two museum security guards stay alert."

"Are your museum security guards armed?"

"Are you kidding? This is Italy. Only the real police are armed."

"Well, then, when they come, the armed cops that are stationed here will stop them. And I'll certainly feel better when they *do* get here. I see you have the paintings ready for shipment. Those are some fancy looking crates."

"Yeah," Iams replied proudly. "There are basically just three sizes—small, medium, and large. All we have to do to get the paintings in the crates is take off the removable endpieces—they're just secured with thumbscrews—and slip the paintings inside."

"Clever. But the exhibition paintings were all different sizes. I saw the exhibit. I can't recall any of them being the same size."

"True. But they did fall into the small, medium, and large categories, no? Sure, the smallest need some stuffing even in the small crates—we use plastic foam blocks as battens. The crates open easy. Come, I'll show you one."

Iams moved to one of the nearest crates and undid the thumbs screws securing the upper end. "This one's a medium," he said, as he lifted off the end and exposed the crate's contents. All Vitelli could see was the frame, and it was held in places by blocks of plastic foam.

"And they're all set up like this?" he asked.

"Pretty much," Iams replied, turning and referring to the remaining eleven crates with a wave of his hand.

Excellent, Vitelli thought, *that makes it easy to slip the transmitter into one.* "Can I see another?"

"Sure," Iams agreed, "but they are all pretty much the same."

"Humor me."

"Okay, if you insist."

As Iams walked away, Vitelli took the tiny transmitter from his pocket, flipped it on, and shoved it deep into one of the foam battens of the open crate in front of him.

"I'll close this one up for you," he said, as Iams began opening one of the larger crates. Vitelli put the end of the crate back in place and tightened down the thumb screws. Then he walked over to the crate Iams had just finished opening, and peered inside. "Yep," he said, "Just as you said—exactly like the other one."

When Iams had resecured that crate, he said, "I wish the policemen who are supposed to be protecting the paintings would show."

"Me too," Vitelli agreed. "Wonder what's keeping them. Giudice said they were supposed to be here."

"What if they don't show?"

"Then that might just prove to be a godsend for the thieves. If the crooks show up in a boat of their own, and if the lighter with Lieutenant Giudice and his men hasn't shown up yet, then there would be no police presence here whatsoever. Then they could very well count on you to just stand by and cooperate."

"And I'd have no choice about that. I would have to do whatever they tell me to, with the vague hope they still won't harm my wife."

"Stinks. Look, I'm going to disappear for a while. Stay outside and see how things play out. As far as you're concerned, I'm not here. Not that you'd let the crooks know I was here anyway."

"Right. Look, Rich, I know these paintings are priceless, and all, but that's not worth you, Donna, or anyone else, getting killed — or even hurt — ever."

"Roger that, Cal. Besides, it's the police contingent's job to put themselves in harm's way — not mine. I'll be careful."

"You do that."

Just then, sirens sounded all over the city.

"What was that?" Vitelli asked.

"Warning sirens," Iams replied. "*Acqua Alta*. High water is coming. They'll begin raising the MOMA barriers soon, closing off the lagoon from the sea, so that they'll be in place at precisely high tide. The sirens are to notify the crews to begin putting out the elevated walkways, and to let the rest of the city know that *Acqua Alta* is coming."

"What would they need the walkways for, if the barriers are deployed and in place?"

"I don't think the Italians completely trust them yet. A couple of times, when they were deployed before, the storm drains backed up, and the streets flooded anyway. Not as badly as if the barriers hadn't been deployed, but there were still almost six inches of water in Saint Mark's Square."

"Just what we need," Vitelli said, "one more complication."

Then there was yet another complication. A gentle rain began to fall.

Chapter 32

Lieutenant Matteo Giudice and four of his men boarded the powered lighter that was to soon leave its berth at the Port of Venice and head for the Oppenheim. Already on board were the lighter's crew: a captain, an engineer, and two mates. It had just started to rain when they shoved off from the quay, and then the sirens sounded.

"*Acqua Alta*," the captain affirmed to a nodding Giudice inside the lighter's wheelhouse; they conversed in Italian. "It should not affect us at all," he said, as he started up the windshield wipers, "even when the tide barriers are lifted. We do not have to leave the lagoon to pick up our cargo, or to transport it to the airport."

"That is a good thing," Matteo replied. "With the barriers erected, there is no access to the Adriatic. The cargo then stays inside the lagoon no matter what."

"Yes," the captain noted, "but they only stay in place for three hours, more or less. So, even if we did have to put to sea, there would only be a minor delay."

"Why only about three hours?"

"Two reasons. First, because that is all that is needed to stem the high tide and keep the city from flooding. And second, because it is the tide that the lagoon depends upon to refresh its waters, and wash any detritus out to sea."

"Detritus?"

The captain smiled. "You *did* know that the city's toilets flush directly into the canals and the lagoon, didn't you?"

"No," Giudice replied. "Actually, I never even thought about it."

"Well, they do. Nobody ever thinks about it. But it was that way in the beginning, fourteen hundred years ago, and it continues to be that way today."

"Really? Honestly, I never, ever thought about it. I guess I always thought the city had a wastewater treatment plant somewhere. *Directly* into the canals, you say? But why then do the canals not stink?"

"Well," the captain smiled, "that is because it is not *directly*. The waste passes through the underground piping first, where it is held and treated naturally inside the piping, just as it might be in a septic tank."

"If you say so. I still will not be tempted to swim in the canals!"

The captain laughed. "Nor I," he said. "I cannot imagine how the city must have stunk when it was first built, when the buildings were higher above the water."

By then, the lighter had pulled out of the channel, and, after rounding the docks and turning to port, it headed east into the Giudecca Canal. Giudice and his men were on the alert, searching the water for a fast-approaching boat, or even men on jet skis.

The lighter was just nearing the canal entrance when the engine quit, and a great clunk was heard emanating from the engine compartment.

"Engineer, what just happened?" the captain called down into the engine spaces.

"I do not know," came the reply. "But it is not good."

An attempt to restart the engine was heard, but the big diesel refused to turn over. By then, the unpowered lighter was drifting south, and outside the ship channel.

"What is going on?" the captain asked again, calling down to the engineer.

"Something is very wrong," the answer came back. "We will not be going anywhere anytime soon. It's the fuel. I just rubbed a bit between my fingers—smelled it. It is not diesel fuel. Someone has filled the tank with gasoline. Must have burnt out the injectors."

"Who could have done that?" the captain asked. "Filled the tank with the wrong fuel?"

"Any idiot, wharf rat," the engineer replied.

"Not just *any* idiot, wharf rat," Giudice observed. "This was sabotage. We were never meant to make it to the museum—and there was never any plan to take over the lighter with an armed attack—obviously, the thieves never planned to engage me and my men, nor let us get anywhere near those paintings! We have been totally fooled!"

It took only a few seconds for him to formulate an alternate plan. "Use your radio. We must mobilize the police boat! We must get me and my men to the museum as quickly as possible!"

"Certainly, Lieutenant," the captain replied, quickly getting on the radio. But then Giudice knew that the police boat might never be mobilized in time for him and his men to get to the museum in time to intercept the thieves. The thieves who, he was certain, were by now headed to the museum in another boat, intending to pick up their loot without interference. He prayed that the force the captain was deploying at the museum would be sufficient to thwart them.

Chapter 33

While Donna Iams dozed off in the locked interior room down the hall, Giorgio, the man called Hulk in the streets, was washing the dinner dishes, the sink basin in front of him full of water. He received a phone call. It was a burner cell phone, and only one other man knew its number. Drying his hands, he answered it.

"Yes, Serb, what is it?"

"I am on the boat, and we are on our way to the museum to pick up the pictures. We do not need the woman any longer. You know what to do."

"Is it really necessary? She's just an old woman. She has hurt no one."

"Do not get all squeamish, now, Hulk. The woman is a liability. She has seen both our faces and can identify us. She must be disposed of."

"I know. But it just seems so cruel."

"Just do it," Serb said, and hung up.

Giorgio took the phone away from his ear and stared at it for a minute or so, before dropping it into the water-filled sink basin.

Chapter 34

Not long after the lighter with Giudice and his men aboard stopped dead in the water, a deep-hulled, sport fishing boat pulled up to the canal landing closest to the entrance of the Oppenheim. It was a fairly large sport fisher, complete with a small skiff mounted on its port side, just aft of the beam. The hull above the water-line and the superstructure had been freshly painted black. The light rain was streaking the paint, exposing the white base beneath.

Out of the boat jumped three armed men, their faces obscured by balaclavas. One of these, a little man who spoke Italian with a strange accent, was the gang's leader, or so it appeared to Vitelli. He had observed the thieves' arrival from a hidden vantage point close to the dock.

Where in the hell are the cops? he wondered. *They should have been here by now. They could have easily taken these three.*

It took no time whatever for the intruders to establish their command of the situation dockside. The unarmed museum guards were quickly subdued after some token resistance; the intruders expected no resistance from Iams, and he proffered none.

The little man barked orders in Italian, and the museum guards began to carry the individual crates from the museum, out onto the dock. Before he allowed any of the crates aboard the boat, however, the little man made the guards open three of them, which he chose at random.

With the poor lighting, and the rain, Vitelli could not imagine what the gang leader was expecting to see inside those particular crates, but as the three crates were opened, he strained his memory to recall exactly which of the crates held the transmitter. *They couldn't be looking for the transmitter,* he reasoned, *or he would make them open every crate.*

Vitelli did know that inside each crate, the painting it contained was cradled in plastic foam battens. With the securing wing nuts removed, and the end of the crate taken off, the painting could be easily slid out of the crate. The reason for the inspection finally came to him. *He wants to check out the paintings themselves! He's sampling the merchandise, making sure Iams hasn't pulled off a switch! I just hope he didn't accidentally select the crate with the transmitter in it!*

Vitelli could see a museum guard grasping the exposed edges of each of the three frames, pulling the individual painting out, and exposing a portion of each one. Despite the poor light, Vitelli could observe the gang leader perfunctorily inspecting the exposed portions of the three paintings, as Iams stood nervously by. In his hiding place, Vitelli let out an anxious breath of his own. *He didn't pick the crate with the transmitter!*

When the gang leader was satisfied, each exposed painting was slid back in place, and the end of its crate reinstalled. Then the other two thieves began loading all twelve of the crates aboard the boat, as the gang leader held a gun on Iams and the two museum guards at dockside.

Vitelli observed this process from his hiding place, still jubilant that at least the thieves had not stumbled upon the hidden radio transmitter.

Still no cops. Where in hell are they? Well, until they arrive – if they ever arrive – I'm going to stick with those paintings. Now, how do I get aboard that boat without being seen? Vitelli knew it was a desperate plan, one he might well have reconsidered, had he just taken the time to think it through.

He watched as the two men loaded the last of the paintings aboard the boat and carried them somewhere belowdecks. Then he watched as Iams spoke to the little man, and heard the man laugh and respond loudly in English. "You want to do *what?*"

Iams then spoke up. "Make sure the paintings are secured. You told me that those were my instructions. Make sure the paintings are stowed securely."

"All right, *Signore* Iams, you and I will go below, and you can inspect how well we have tied the crates down. Meanwhile, I will see to it that these others will not bother us anytime soon." The gang leader then spoke to the two others in Italian, and they escorted the two museum guards back inside the museum.

Vitelli watched, and as soon as Iams and his escort boarded the sport fisher and went below, he quietly braved the rain and slipped aboard the boat. Once aboard, he searched for a place to hide. He found a padded seat in the stern of the boat that opened into a storage bin. Inside the bin were some coils of rope, some other odds and ends, and barely enough room for him. He lay down inside anyway, and pulled the lid down. With the lid closed, he noted that a series of holes had been drilled horizontally across the upper part of the bin wall, holes which let in the meagre light. *Probably for ventilation,* he thought, *but also good for some very limited vision onto the deck and to hear what's going on.* There was also something else, something sharp, sticking him in his ribs. He shifted away from it as best he could, and tried to ignore it. *At least I'm out of the rain.*

"Are you satisfied, *Signore* Iams?" Vitelli heard the little man with the strange accent address Iams as they emerged from somewhere below.

"I am," Iams said. "You said that you would harm my wife if I didn't make sure the paintings were secured."

"And, so I did," the man said with amusement. "And so you did, too. Now you will be brought inside and tied up with the others. Your cooperation will not go unnoticed, *Signore* Iams. Your wife will be just fine."

About five minutes later, Vitelli estimated, the three thieves returned to the boat, the engine was started, and he could feel it in motion as the boat pulled out into the canal and started moving forward.

Chapter 35

Anubis Cline had spent a busy day aboard the borrowed yacht. His business dealings were such that he could conduct them from anywhere, just so long as he had a secure Internet connection. In that regard, at least, the yacht was well equipped. His only difficulty was the need to adjust to operating from a different time zone. His business with the Far East had, of course, to be done on that area's time schedule. He was used to being awake and operating at odd hours back in the city, and while the times he had to be online hadn't changed in absolute terms, here across the Atlantic they *felt* different; and that perception, he worried, might just throw him off his game.

I worry, Jael, and I fear it might be affecting my health.

"*How so, Abba?*"

I am logy. And I'm not sleeping all that well. Back home, I could contact Hong Kong at the start of business at seven in the evening. Here, I must call at two in the morning. India is another problem altogether. While it really is all straightforward, it's also quite confusing the same time. My body clock is all off.

"*Ah, now I understand.*"

Yes, and the sooner this business here is over and done with, the sooner you and I can both go back home.

"It should all be over soon. The paintings should be aboard in a matter of hours. Just think – a dozen paintings, each worth millions."

I adore your enthusiasm, but, well, not really. The collectors I have lined up to buy them know full well that they were stolen, and will never pay market value for any of them. After all, one can hardly hang a stolen Picasso or a pilfered Monet on one's living room wall, can one?

"No, not hardly. But you have earmarked The Starry Night for yourself. What will you do with it?"

Well, I will just own it! Lock it up in the vault and take it out and admire it from time to time. That is most likely the same thing the others I will sell to will do!

"Hardly rational, don't you think, Abba?"

Cline grunted; for him, that was a laugh. No, my dear, not at all rational – not rational in the least! But satisfying, eh?

With his mind's eye, Cline could see his ward smile her approval.

Chapter 36

Justino Carrillo had already begun issuing orders to deploy the MOSE barriers. It was important that all three of the entrances to the lagoon off the Adriatic be sealed off well before the high tide.

Each barrier caisson was raised from the sea floor by opening the blow valve that admitted compressed air into each individual unit, pushing out the water that held it down, and allowing it to rise, on its tether, to the surface. The individual blow valves were each controlled from the main panel at the control center in the *Arsenale*.

Carrillo started at the Lido entrance first.

The procedure was to raise every other caisson first, then fill in the gaps, one at a time, until all the caissons were interlocked together, forming a watertight barrier between the high water in the Adriatic, and the lower water level in the lagoon

Carrillo had just ordered the first of the second set of Lido gap caissons to be deployed, when the black sport fisher approached one of the gaps between the caissons already in place, at speed.

The men deployed at the Lido gap, there to observe the barrier deployment, saw the black shape approach out of the night, and with lights and shouts, attempted to wave it off. But to no avail. The boat's steel hull could be heard scraping its starboard side along the edge of one of the caissons, as it bridged, then sped through, the gap.

When he heard what had happened, Carrillo was furious. He ordered inspection of the caisson that had been struck (they are designed to interlock carefully, one with the other, after all, or the system would not work). There was no telling how much damage the marauding boat night have done, or how it might affect the functioning of the barrier system.

Carrillo resolved to call the Italian Coast Guard, also stationed in the *Arsenale,* and issue a formal complaint, even though it would do little good. The interloper would, after all, be long gone to only-God-knows-where, whenever he could stop what he was doing long enough to report it — but report it to the *Guardia Costiera* he would.

Chapter 37

It took some time for the police patrol boat to reach the stranded lighter, and for Giudice and his men to transfer to it. Once aboard, though, the boat proceeded at speed, lights flashing and siren wailing, down the Giudecca Canal. It then made its way around the *Punta della Dogana,* and the church of Santa Maria Salute, and into the Grand Canal at its easternmost entrance, just opposite St. Mark's Square. From there, it was only a short way down to the Oppenheim, but, still, it was already past 1:00 AM.

With the lights and the siren off, the police boat approached dockside at the Oppenheim. It was dark along the quay, and it was still raining. The quay was empty as the patrol boat reached it, and then tied up. Giudice ordered his men off the boat and had them surround the museum. They tried all the doors, then, finding the back door to the museum workshop unlocked, they used it to enter the museum. There, in the workshop, they found Iams and the two museum guards tied up and gagged.

"What time is it?" Iams asked, as soon as his gag came off.

"It is zero-one-fifteen," Giudice answered.

"They left just after midnight. Leave us! If you hurry, you may be able to catch them."

"They will not get far," Giudice said, sounding confident. "The MOSE barriers are already being deployed. They cannot leave the lagoon."

"I hope you're right," Iams replied. "Their boat looked sleek and fast. If they manage to get out to sea, they will be hard to catch."

"That's if they are even headed out to sea. But if they are, and do manage to get into the Adriatic, then we can launch the department helicopter." *If Vitelli managed to put that transmitter in with the paintings,* he thought, *that boat should not be too hard to locate.* "Where is Vitelli, and what happened to the police officers who were stationed here?"

"There were no police officers here. They never showed. And I have no idea where Vitelli is. He said he was going to stay back, hide, and observe — get involved only if he thought he could accomplish something."

"Then he must still be around here someplace. As for why my men never showed, that I cannot explain. Captain Benedetto assured me that there would be four men here well before midnight."

"Well, they never showed."

"So you said. I wonder why not?" Giudice asked rhetorically.

Chapter 38

Giorgio had brought Donna Iams a particularly nice dinner: veal scallopini marsala with a delicate mushroom sauce; bright green broccoli, cooked through, but still crisp; and a side of pasta in an oil and garlic sauce. There was also a bottle of domestic red wine. Everything was so good that Donna somewhat overindulged. The wine made her sleepy, so she decided to lie down only for a minute. It was the sirens that woke her up.

"What is that all about?" she wondered aloud, and, looking across the room, discovered that Giorgio must have come by while she was asleep, and had cleaned up and removed the dirty dishes.

Donna also had to pee, and thought to call out to Giorgio to let her out of the room to use the bathroom. But when she looked toward the door, she became confused. The door to her prison room was wide open. She left the room and made the familiar trip down the hall to the bathroom. When she emerged, she thought to call out to Giorgio, but decided to explore instead.

She found the kitchen and the living spaces, even Giorgio's bedroom, which he apparently shared with that other, disagreeable fellow. But neither one was anywhere to be seen. She descended a stairway, and tried what she thought might be the front door to the place, and opened it. She found herself out on the street, or, rather, the *fondamento* of a canal.

The night air was cool, the sky cloudy, and a gentle rain was falling. The ground was wet from the rain, and there were shallow puddles here and there. She thought for a second to retreat back into the building. *No*, she quickly decided, *I'm never going back in there. I'd rather get wet than be locked up again!*

Donna tried to think back and remember which way they had taken when Giorgio and the man called Serb had brought her here. But it was dark out, and the streets were not that well-lit, and she became confused. *But this is Venice*, she thought, *and if I just keep walking, I'm bound to come upon something or someplace I recognize.*

So, Donna just started walking.

Giorgio had just enough money left over, after buying the veal cutlets at the butcher shop, for the second-class ticket to Naples. While Donna Iams was wandering the wet city streets to his east, he sat in the southbound train awaiting its departure. In Italy, and indeed throughout Europe, trains run pretty much on time. And his train, he knew, would leave the station in just five minutes. Then he would be well away from Serb, their boss Charlie, and all the rest of this nasty business. He may well be, after all, a thief, but he was *not* a murderer.

Chapter 39

Vitelli stayed quiet in his hidey-hole in the stern of the fishing boat. He had been unable to hear or see very much, but the boat's sudden stutter, and the screech as the hull scraped along the caisson, he had heard well enough. Despite the screech, however, the boat continued to run at full speed for a good while afterward. Then it slowed, and finally came to a complete stop.

Vitelli didn't know it, but the boat was at a dead stop in the Adriatic. What he *did* know was that the boat began to wallow in the swells, and that he was starting to feel queasy. He had served aboard a destroyer in the Navy, and had never gotten seasick. But in the Navy, he had never been confined to a tight space, wearing wet clothing, aboard a small vessel wallowing at dead stop.

Vitelli was thinking about the impending necessity of leaving his hiding place when, through one of the airholes, he saw two men come out on deck. He heard one of the men speaking Italian with a strange accent say something to the other, as both men peered over the boat's starboard side.

Must have been what that screeching was all about, scaping the hull on something, Vitelli thought. Then the two men straightened up, apparently satisfied with their inspection, and he heard the one man say something to the other. One word was repeated several times, a word whose meaning was clear in any language *"il transmittente."*

Shit! That has to mean "transmitter." The bastards know I've hidden a transmitter in with the paintings. How in hell could they have found that out? Not even Iams knew about it. Shit!

Then both men left the deck, one returning to the cabin, the other disappearing somewhere else.

Probably going belowdecks to look for that transmitter. Vitelli heard the engine below rumbling to life again, felt the boat vibrate, and soon the boat was once again traveling fast—but to where, Vitelli had no clue. He could only surmise that the boat was now somewhere well outside the lagoon and in the Adriatic.

Vitelli lifted the lid of his hidey-hole, and quietly got out onto the deck, and stepped into a cold breeze. The rain, he noted thankfully, had stopped. He crouched there by the box in the stern for a full minute, getting his bearings.

He looked up into the night sky. The clouds he had observed in the city earlier were gone, the waning moon was down on the horizon, and he could see the bright panoply of stars overhead. He had briefly studied celestial navigation in OCS (Officer Candidate School) and had even done some practice "Day's Work in Navigation" required of all Naval officers serving aboard ship. But, in actual practice, the ship's navigator ignored the stars entirely at sea, and relied entirely on GPS.

I really don't have a clue where we are going, or even in which direction we're headed. The North Star—where is it?

Wait a sec. Boy Scouts — the two stars on the end of The Big Dipper's "cup" point the way. And the north star is the last star in the handle of The Little Dipper. He searched, and to his surprise easily located both constellations and the star itself, off the left side of the boat, not quite off the beam, but a point or so forward of it.

He then realized that just below the star was a bloom of light, well off in the distance, just beyond the horizon. This, again, was off the port side of the boat. *There are shore lights off to the left, so, there are people and land over there. North Adriatic coastline, got to be. That has to mean we're headed east-northeast, probably in the direction of . . . Trieste.*

He then resolved to find his way belowdecks where the paintings were stowed. Somehow, unarmed though he was, he needed to stop these guys from finding and silencing that transmitter.

Chapter 40

Donna Iams wandered a bit, and crossed over several waterways, almost unconsciously moving from the more dimly-lit parts of the city to parts with better lighting. She looked for the signs posted on the corners of the buildings directing tourists to places of interest, but saw none. There were street signs, but she recognized none of the names.

She eventually found herself on a street named *Strada Nuova*, or "New Street," and, where it crossed over a canal, sighted down the canal in both directions. To the left, was another crossing bridge; to the right was what she recognized as the Grand Canal. She continued forward, and now there were some people—people setting up some elevated walkways—people who studiously ignored the wet little old lady dressed in the rumpled blue pants suit.

Donna knew well what the walkways were for: *Acqua Alta*. It was just what she needed right now. Not only was it raining, and she didn't know where she was, but she might have to contend with flooded streets as well.

She stopped someone who looked like she might be a native, and, in her excellent Italian, asked her for the direction of Saint Mark's. The woman looked at her strangely, and pointed down the street.

"Continua a camminare in quella direzione," she said, still pointing down the street.

"Grazie," Donna replied, and kept walking in the direction the woman indicated. As she walked, crossing over three more smaller canals, the street became more and more populated, mostly with the walkway setters. The street also became better and better lit. The crowd was also thickening, with both walkway setters and now night-owl tourists. Then, to her happy surprise, she arrived at the foot of the Rialto Bridge. Now she knew exactly where she was, and strode with purpose to the south, and toward the Accademia Bridge.

Chapter 41

The more he thought about it, the more Vitelli kicked himself for getting on the boat to begin with. It was, he realized, his unwillingness to let the thieves get away Scot free with the paintings that prompted the move, but it was still a boneheaded play.

Before he did anything else, he now knew he had to arm himself with a weapon of some kind. He looked around. *This is a fishing boat, there must be something!* Then he remembered that "something sharp" that stuck him in the ribs in his hidey-hole. Going back to the box, he lifted the padded seat. There was the thing that had stuck him: a fishing gaff, one with a nasty-looking, metal hook mounted on the end of a thick wooden shaft, about three-and-a-half-feet long. *Not exactly a gun,* he considered, *but something, at least!*

Now, duly armed, Vitelli made his way forward, doing his best to move quietly and stay out of the feeble light that outlined the boat's superstructure. Up in the wheelhouse, he could see the back of the man driving the boat. He quietly entered the cabin door below the wheelhouse, hoping to find his way belowdecks, and discover the hold where the paintings had been stowed.

A short passage led to another, longer passage, that led both fore and aft along the boat. He heard some rummaging behind a door forward. *That's probably where the paintings are, and that noise is probably the guy searching for the transmitter.*

He slowly made his way forward as stealthily as he could, when suddenly the door forward slammed open, and a man came storming down upon him, shouting *"L'ho trovato!* (I found it!) *L'ho trovato!"*

The man must have been just as surprised as Vitelli was, but his reactions were a lot quicker. Before Vitelli could raise the gaff for a strike, the man hit him square in the jaw with his fist, and, for Vitelli, the lights immediately went out.

When Vitelli came to, he was back above decks, but flat on his back. His hands were tied behind him, and his feet were tied together as well.

The smaller of the two men he had spied earlier stood over him. *"Chi Sei?* he asked. When he got a blank stare from Vitelli, he tried *"Wir bist du?"* Still no reaction. Finally, he asked, "Who are you?"

"Vitelli," he answered. "My name is Vitelli."

Vitelli noted the man's slight build, narrow pock-marked face, dark eyes, and prominent nose. His English was strangely accented. The man behind him, the one who hit him, was tall, young, athletic-looking. A handsome kid, actually, with wavy black hair and dark eyes. "And what are you doing on my boat, Vitelli?" the man asked.

"I'm working with the Italian authorities. I stowed away when I saw you load the paintings aboard. I wanted to be there when the police catch up with you, whoever you are."

"I am called Serb, not that you will ever tell anyone. So? You wanted to be there when they catch us? Fat chance of their finding us now, my friend. My man, Marco, here, had just found your clever little radio transmitter, when you surprised him. Really, Vitelli, did you expect an old man like yourself, even armed with a fishing gaff, to be a match for a young stud like Marco?"

Vitelli remained silent.

"And as for the *carabinieri* finding us," Serb continued to brag, "they never will. That transmitter, you see, is now securely aboard this boat's skiff, which only moments ago we set adrift. If the cops are looking for that transmitter signal, they will be very surprised when they do find it—if they *ever* do—which they probably never will, because the police boat cannot leave the Venice lagoon. Not, at least, until the flood barriers are lowered. How fortunate for us that *Acqua Alta* arrived just when it did! And if you're thinking about the police helicopter, this is Italy, after all, and it will take some time to get it mobilized, and into the air. By that time, they still will never find us. Nor, I think, will they ever find you—stupid, stupid, *Signore* Vitelli!"

"*I'm* stupid? How about *you*, mastermind? Exactly how do you plan to sell those paintings? Not exactly something you sell on the open market!"

"Not my problem, Vitelli. I am, you see, no mastermind. I leave all the masterminding to others. My job was only to steal the paintings and get them to Trieste and to the *real* mastermind — the man my boss, Charlie, calls 'Reaper,' who wants them so badly, the American who is bankrolling this entire little adventure. No, and Charlie, my boss, is no mastermind, either — just another underling like myself, one who sees to it that stealing the paintings happens easily and without any police interference. It was my boss, Charlie, who insured the complete cooperation of *Signore* Calvin Iams, the man who was responsible for crating and transporting the paintings back to America."

"So, it wasn't your idea to kidnap Donna Iams, Serb?"

"No, it was entirely the idea of my boss," he laughed. "Charlie is the one who creates opportunities and removes obstacles. What is the English word for that?"

Vitelli thought for a second. "Facilitator," he offered.

"Yes, exactly. My boss, Charlie, is a *facilitator*, Vitelli. It was Charlie who directed that we should kidnap *Signora* Iams, and make sure that *Signore* Iams would not pose any problems for our little adventure. And it was Charlie who told me there would be a transmitter hidden among the paintings."

How in blazes did this Charlie guy find out about the transmitter? Vitelli wondered. Aloud, he asked, "And *Signora* Iams, what will happen to her?"

"Unfortunately for the *Signora*, Vitelli, she has seen our faces and can identify me and Hulk, my associate. So, unfortunately, she cannot be allowed to live. If she has not already been found, then she still floats in one of the interior Venetian canals."

"You Bastards! Donna Iams would never hurt anybody!" Vitelli strained against his bonds.

Vitelli then heard the unpleasant little man issue some orders in Italian to the man, Marco, who had surprised him below. Marco then picked him up as easily as he would pick up a small sack of potatoes, and tossed him over the stern, and into the sea.

Chapter 42

Giudice had enough presence of mind to call ahead and see if the MOSE barriers had already have been raised. He found out that they had indeed already been raised, and would stay in place for the better part of another three hours. All boat traffic this side of the barriers was now locked up inside the lagoon. Chasing the thieves in the police boat was, obviously, out of the question.

Time, Giudice reasoned, was of the essence. He could not just cool his heels until the barrier came down. He needed to do something *now*, something that would enable his overtaking the thieves' boat, and recovering the paintings.

There was the police helicopter. It was hangered at the tiny Lido airport, and could be in the air, practically speaking, in about an hour — possibly longer. That was, of course, after he had first cleared its use with Captain Benedetto, who was, more than likely, at home with his sick wife.

On second thought, Giudice reasoned, *the police helicopter is small, and can only hold a pilot and three passengers. Even if we could locate the thieves' boat, we could do little more than just follow it. No, something bigger is needed, something with a bigger punch.*

Then it occurred to him: The *Guardia Costiera* — the Italian Coast Guard! They had a base at the Arsenal, and they had a rescue helicopter, always gassed up and at the ready!

"Head for the Coast Guard Base at the Arsenal," he told the policeboat coxswain in Italian, "while I radio ahead and make the arrangements."

After identifying himself, and explaining his emergency, he begged the Coast Guard Duty Officer to deploy their helicopter to chase the thieves. He explained that he had a receiver for the transmitter that had been hidden away with stolen art treasures worth millions, and that he could be at the *Guardia Costiera* station in just a few minutes.

Giudice got lucky. The duty officer had been the same person to whom Justino Carrillo has spoken earlier, reporting the marauding, black, fishing boat that had breached the MOSE barrier, and which had damaged one of the caissons. Connecting that incident with this new one, the duty officer told Giudice to come ahead. The helicopter was being readied then, and it could take off as soon as Giudice could get there.

But the duty officer had been somewhat optimistic. When Giudice arrived at the base, the helicopter was nowhere near ready to deploy: the pilot and his crew had only recently been roused, and were still getting their gear together. The bird itself had been flown during the previous day, and had not yet been refueled. But at least it had stopped raining.

Some seventy minutes later, Giudice was airborne in the fully-crewed rescue helicopter. They had just cleared the airspace over the still-deployed Lido entry MOSE barrier, and were heading out over the Adriatic.

Giudice had to assume that Vitelli had successfully stowed that transmitter in with the paintings. But what had happened to Vitelli? He was nowhere near the museum, and Giudice couldn't take the time to search for him. He didn't know what hotel he and Pam were staying in, but wouldn't call there anyway, lest he panic Pam needlessly. It occurred to Giudice that Vitelli may have foolishly snuck aboard that boat, but he hoped he was wrong.

Now airborne, this was his near-impossible mission: to search and locate a faint transmission from a radio transmitter hopefully hidden aboard a boat, and find twelve paintings worth millions; and maybe also find an American cop-turned-tourist named Vitelli, who may well have idiotically stowed himself aboard.

Chapter 43

Growing up, Vitelli was never all that comfortable in the water. He could swim, but he was never very good at it, and tired out easily. When he decided to apply for Navy Officer Candidate School, the idea of having to take, and pass, the Navywide, Third Class swim test, gave him some concern. He had read through the requirements: jump into the water from a height of ten feet; float for five minutes; swim for fifty yards; trap air in your clothing and use it as a flotation device.

The thing that really gave him some pause was the floating part; try as he might, he could never float for very long. He always seemed to exhaust himself fighting to remain on the surface. He seriously doubted he could float by himself for five minutes, without the aid of some flotation device.

So, before applying for OCS, Vitelli enrolled in a Red Cross swimming class. There he quickly improved his swimming technique, learning to better coordinate his breathing with his stroke. But he still had problems with floating—at least until his instructor, Chuck (Vitelli never knew his last name), took him aside for some one-on-one training. Chuck, a retired Navy SEAL, took a shine to Vitelli when he learned his student was planning to join the Navy.

Like most people, Vitelli was a "floater," but never knew it. The average person has three to four pounds of positive buoyancy in the water when their lungs are fully inflated, and they will not start to sink until they exhale completely.

Chuck taught him to relax, arch his back, lean back with his mouth out of the water, and to keep his lungs full of air. Then he went one step further: he taught Vitelli the Drownproofing Survival Technique.

"In drownproofing," Chuck explained, "you float almost vertically face down in the water, with only the top of your head above the surface. Using your arms and legs, you exert a downward pressure, lifting your mouth out of the water; take a breath, and then fall back into a relaxed float. Try it," he suggested.

Vitelli's first efforts were a disaster. He kept sucking in air too soon, as he lifted his head out of the water, and aspirating half the pool. "You're panicking," Chuck would say. "Relax. Now try again."

And when he did, Vitelli was eventually able to remain afloat comfortably for several minutes. "The thing," Chuck kept reiterating, "is not to panic. To relax, and stay relaxed. Hell, in SEAL training, we did this with our legs tied together and our hands tied behind our back."

"And how did that work?" Vitelli asked.

"Not as easily as with your arms and legs available, kid, obviously, but the drown proofing technique still worked. You just had to modify the method a little. You use a dolphin kick—you know—where you kind of undulate, holding your legs together, and push with your legs and whole lower body. Here, I'll show you." Then he demonstrated, his hands held behind his back, and his legs clamped together.

"We could keep it up for hours, and did," Chuck continued. "Admittedly, it was in an indoor pool like this one, in ideal conditions, and under constant surveillance. And I was, of course, in much, much, better shape."

"You make it look so easy," Vitelli said, and, holding his hands behind his back, and clamping his legs together, tried it himself. However, within minutes, he was again coughing and spitting, swimming hard to grab the edge of the pool.

Chuck laughed. "Takes a bit of practice," he said, "and, again, you panicked."

Several weeks later, in Newport, Rhode Island, the Navy Third Class swim test was administered during Vitelli's first week in OCS. For the "five minutes floating" part, Vitelli used the drownproofing flotation technique Chuck had shown him, and he had been practicing in the Red Cross pool since. He passed the swim test with flying colors. But that was the last time he had any reason to use the drownproofing technique. Twelve weeks later, he was commissioned as an ensign in the Navy, having finished third in his graduating class.

That was some twenty years earlier, and now Vitelli found himself thrown into the cold Adriatic Sea, again coughing and spitting, with his feet tied together, and his hands tied behind his back. But there was no solid pool wall here to grab hold of here, no place to take refuge.

Chuck's voice screamed at him from over the years: **"Don't panic! Relax!"** Not until he swallowed a mouthful of seawater, did Vitelli force himself to do just those things.

First fill your lungs with air. Getting vertical in the water, he dolphin-kicked to the surface, gulped in air, then settled back into the sea. Thankfully, he noted, the water is relatively calm, just long, easy swells. *Vertical float. Exhale, kick back, head up and out, take a breath, settle back. Repeat.* Vitelli was far too busy to remark on the black fishing boat, paintings aboard, speeding away to the east. *Lose the shoes,* he thought, and kicked them off.

Exhale, kick back, head up and out, take a breath, settle back. Repeat. Exhale, kick back, head up and out, take a breath, settle back. Repeat.

At least the water wasn't all that cold. After the initial shock, he had adjusted to the water temperature; it was slightly warmer than the air temperature, or so it seemed. Still, any water temperature below body temperature sucked off body heat, and water was far more efficient at doing that than air. Between the drownproofing routine, and the water sucking off his body heat, Vitelli knew he could only last so long before total exhaustion overtook him, and he would just fall fatally asleep.

Exhale, kick back, head up and out, take a breath, settle back. Repeat. Exhale, kick back, head up and out, take a breath, settle back. Repeat.

Much easier if I could use my arms. Maybe if I pulled my knees up to my chest, then I could pull my hands around under my feet. He did, holding his breath, and went into a summersault. Still, he managed to pass his hands under his feet. *Don't panic!* he thought, and managed to right himself, kick out of the water, and get some precious air.

Exhale, kick back, head up and out, take a breath, settle back. Repeat. Exhale, kick back, head up and out, take a breath, settle back. Repeat.

Much easier with my hands in front of me. Have to work on that knot. And he did, whenever he was holding his breath, and when his mouth was under the surface, biting at the knot. But with no success.

Exhale, kick back, head up and out, take a breath, settle back. Repeat. Exhale, kick back, head up and out, take a breath, settle back. Repeat.

Chapter 44

Back at the Oppenheim, Donna Iams had just completed her trek across the city and had crossed over the Accademia Bridge. The museum was quiet; nobody was in the street outside, yet all the lights in the building itself were on. She found her way inside the museum through the rear entrance, and found her husband sitting sullenly in an armless chair in the museum workshop. That changed immediately when he caught sight of her. "Donna!" he exclaimed. "Thank God! You're alive!"

"So it would appear," she said, smiling broadly, as her husband rushed up to embrace her, wet clothes and all.

After some hugging and kissing, Iams admitted, "I thought I might never see you again. Oh, Donna! I didn't know what to do! And I took such a chance!"

"Whatever do you mean?" she asked.

And he showed her.

Chapter 45

Once the *Guardia Costiera* helicopter was out over the Adriatic, the pilot asked Giudice in Italian, "Which way?"

And Giudice had to think for a moment. Once past the Lido entry barrier, the thieves could have headed in just about any direction, but the two most likely directions were west-northwest in the direction of Trieste, or south, down the Italian peninsula, toward any one of a number of destinations.

Where would I go with millions of dollars of stolen paintings aboard? Giudice thought. *Someplace where I could unload them quickly, no doubt, for transfer to another vessel, perhaps, or onto an aircraft. Any number of places along Italy's Adriatic coast would fit the bill, but then the paintings would remain in Italy, and under Italian jurisdiction. No, better across the Adriatic, land on Italian soil perhaps, but still be close on to the Balkans. There they could disappear forever.*

"Go east," Giudice told the pilot in Italian. "And stay close to the coastline. I am betting that whoever is driving that fishing boat is inexperienced, and not all that comfortable away from the coast—that the boat's ultimate destination is anywhere the crooks could unload the paintings for transport into Slovenia or Croatia."

"That would be toward Trieste, then," the pilot said.

"Toward Trieste, then, it is," replied Giudice, realizing he was betting a great deal on an educated guess.

Giudice glanced at the radio receiver in his hand. The transmitter, he knew had a limited range—five kilometers at most; they would have to be practically on top of the paintings to receive its transmission. *We are, I'm afraid, on a fool's errand. But there is nothing else for it. We have to try and find that boat—and Vitelli, if he did board that boat, and hasn't been discovered and murdered by now.*

Chapter 46

Vitelli had no idea how long he had been in the water. It may have been a matter of minutes, but it certainly seemed like hours. All he was sure of was that he was getting tired—very tired.

Exhale, kick back, head up and out, take a breath, settle back. Repeat. Exhale, kick back, head up and out, take a breath, settle back. Repeat.

Then, when he lifted his head out of the water to take a breath, he saw a gray shape looming faintly off in the distance. *A buoy!* he thought, and without considering why a buoy might be anywhere near where he was, he decided he had to swim to it. *Something to hang onto, at least.*

He swam toward the shape as best he could. His hands were still tied (he had not managed to loosen the knot, no matter how hard he tried) as were his legs. He did a kind of breast stroke, using his arms to push on the water when it came time to lift his head up and out to breathe, coupled with a dolphin kick. But it was slow and sloppy, and his limbs were like lead. Still, he seemed to make some progress. It even seemed as if the shape was actually moving towards him, meeting him halfway. Then he saw it was not a buoy at all, but a small boat. *It's the skiff off the fishing boat! I have to get to it. I have to!*

Suddenly, the boat was on top of him, looking as if it might just drift by before he could reach it. With a Herculean effort, Vitelli pushed himself up and out of the water and grabbed the side of the skiff. Holding on, he rested for a while, and then pulled himself slowly aboard. In tipping the side to him, the boat took on some water, but not enough to sink it. Once aboard the skiff, Vitelli relaxed.

Inside the boat, duct-taped to the opposite gunwale, was a tiny metal box. *The transmitter,* Vitelli thought, and then fell into an exhausted sleep

Chapter 47

The fishing boat was well on its way to its rendezvous with Cline's borrowed yacht in Trieste. In another four hours or so, Serb mused, they would be transferring their peculiar cargo to the yacht, and he would be collecting a fat paycheck — or that, at least was the plan.

Serb was indeed the suspicious type. He really was Serbian, born Felip Ilić, but he grew up in Bosnia, in a Serbian conclave, in the 1990s. As a child, he contracted a disfiguring skin disease that left him scarred for life. Those were turbulent times.

It was in the '90s that Serbia's Slobodan Milosevic invaded the country of little Felip's birth. Milosevic's stated objective was to "free" ethnic Serbians, Orthodox Christians like Serb himself, from the tyranny of their Muslim neighbors. Except that, until Milosevic invaded Bosnia, the Bosnian Muslims and Christians had been living peacefully, side by side, without incident, some even in integrated neighborhoods.

To complicate matters, Croatians, also living in Bosnia, with the backing of Croatia, used the invasion as an excuse to seek their own republic. It was a mess, with neighbor suddenly turning against neighbor.

Serb, barely a teenager, watched his entire family slaughtered by a Muslim militia. To survive, he learned to lie and cheat and steal. But survive he did, and eventually made his way west, falling almost naturally into a career of crime.

Now Serb was to deliver his precious cargo to Reaper, the man Charlie had said was the brains of their operation. Nobody, not even Charlie, knew the real identity of this Reaper person, other than he had to be some rich American eccentric, living on a yacht in Trieste. He had bankrolled their operation generously thus far, and there would be, for Serb, an astronomical payout, once the paintings were delivered intact. Serb had been tasked to ensure that delivery; he was also to be the one to witness the wire transfer of Reaper's payout to Charlie's numbered account in a San Marino bank.

Of course, Charlie would get the lion's share of the payout. No way Serb was happy about that. But Charlie, after all, had taken the greatest risk, and the hundred-thousand euros Serb and his gang would be paid was, after all, not a bad day's wage.

Still, much could yet go wrong, and there was no way to be sure that this Reaper person would live up to his part of the bargain. Of course, Serb was armed. And Serb was not at all squeamish about using his 9mm Russian Baikal pistol if the situation demanded it.

Chapter 48

As the Coast Guard helicopter made its way on a more or less easterly course across the Adriatic, Giudice, seated next to the pilot, scanned the horizon. There was some scant traffic, mostly small boats, and coastal lighters in tow. He strained to catch a glimpse of the thieves' fishing boat. Every once in a while, Giudice would glance at the diminutive radio receiver he held balanced in his lap. It was supposed to flash a light, and beep, when it received a signal. A signal from the transmitter that he hoped had been hidden in among the stolen paintings. But, so far, nothing. But, then, they hadn't been in the air for all that long.

"How far out do you think we are now, Captain?" he asked in Italian, speaking into the microphone of the headset attached to the borrowed helmet he wore. The mike gave him network communication over the roar of the engine, not only with the pilot, but also to the two crewmembers who rode the jump seats in the open, back section of the helicopter cockpit.

"Not far at all," the pilot replied in the same language. "We are just over twenty kilometers or so from the Arsenal base. If the boat we are chasing is making any speed at all, then they are still way ahead of us. Relax,

Lieutenant. Assuming we are heading in the same direction as they are, then we still have —"

He was interrupted by the flash of light and the beep that came from the transmitter in Giudice's lap.

"They have got to be close!" Giudice exclaimed.

"Where, then?" the pilot answered. "There is no boat in sight — wait — what is that down there?"

"Where?"

"Down there," the pilot said, pointing. "Cannot possibly be our guys, though. That is no full-size fishing boat. Hell, it is no more than a little punt. Still, it appears to be the source of the radio transmission."

One of the two coastguardsmen in the back, having heard the conversation, said, "I can see it too, Captain. Shall I light it up, so we can get a better look?"

"Do that, Alonzo. I will hover over the boat and you put the spotlight on it." The bright beam of light from the hovering helicopter lit up a man sprawled inside the skiff below. He was not moving, and did not appear to be aware of either the bright light, or the machine flying directly over him.

"There is someone inside that boat, Captain, and he does not look so good."

"I can see that, Alonzo. It looks like we may have to go into rescue mode. See if you can get any response out of him with the loudhailer."

"In barca, tutto bene?" the call went out over the loudhailer. Nothing. The figure below did not move.

"Go and get him, Alonzo," the pilot ordered.

There was then a flurry of activity in the back of the helicopter, the two coastguardsmen rigging out a hoist off the port side of the machine. The man called Alonzo stripped down to his underwear and put on a wet suit, a diving mask, and snorkel. "We are ready, Captain," he reported.

"Okay, Alonzo, I will bring you in close." The pilot then brought the craft down directly over the floating skiff. The machine's updraft filled the air with large drop-lets of saltwater rain. Alonzo jumped the fifteen feet or so that separated the hovering helicopter from the sur-face, landing in the sea just about two yards from the skiff. Somehow, Giudice noted, he managed to enter the water without his head ever going below the surface. And now Giudice recognized the man in the skiff.

"The man in the boat," he reported over the network, "that is the American policeman. That is Lieutenant Vi-telli!"

Minutes later the hoist brought Vitelli and his rescuer aboard the helicopter. "He is alive, but unconscious, and barely breathing," Alonzo reported as he came aboard. "He is in bad shape. His hands and feet are tied together. And they are *very* cold. He needs medical attention. We can warm him up some and maybe get him on oxygen, but he needs to see a doctor."

The two coastguardsmen immediately went to work on Vitelli, quickly cutting through the ropes that bound his hands and feet, then swaddling him in blankets. They took his vital signs. "He definitely has hypothermia," one reported, putting an oxygen mask over Vitelli's face.

"Looks like we head back to Venice, Lieutenant," the pilot said, turning his craft back to the west. "Sorry about your fishing boat escaping, but we have to do our best to save this man's life."

"No, Captain, you are right, of course. Vitelli's life — any man's life — is worth far more than all the art in Venice."

Still, a part of Giudice deeply regretted letting that fishing boat get away.

Chapter 49

Five hours after Vitelli was transported to a Venetian hospital, the sport fisher, with the three thieves aboard, and twelve crates of paintings in the forward hold, pulled into the harbor at Trieste.

Serb's instructions were to pull into the Yacht Club Adriaco, there to locate a large white yacht out of Abu Dhabi, named "Zayed." The weather was somewhat like it had been when they left Venice, but more so: cloudier, windier, colder, but with no rain. The first blush of dawn had appeared over the city over an hour earlier, but it was still early, and there were very few people about in the marina.

While the hundred-meter yacht was impressive, Serb had expected to find a much larger craft. He pulled alongside, and, again, as instructed, hailed the Zayed: "*Charlie chiede il permesso di affiancarsi,*" or, "Charlie requests permission to come alongside." When nothing happened, he again yelled out, all the louder, "***Charlie chiede il permesso di affiancarsi!***"

Another minute or so later, heads appeared over the yacht's railing, and fenders were let down over the side of the yacht and secured. These were followed by mooring lines passed to the fishing boat. Next, a Jacob's ladder was lowered into the boat.

With the fishing boat securely tied up alongside, Serb climbed up the Jacob's ladder and hauled himself over the yacht's railing. Once aboard, he noted that the yacht was more impressive than it had appeared from alongside. Its lines were sweeping and sleek, its brass appointments brightly polished, the deck freshly holy stoned teak. Up overhead, were three more levels. The topmost level, was the control house, and its roof bristled with the evidence of the latest electronic equipment—radar dishes, aerials, antennae of every stripe.

Serb was greeted in English by a scowling, sour-faced, man with a long, sharp nose, and beady black eyes. He wore what appeared to be some sort of uniform: blue suit jacket, white trousers and shoes, and a white cap. Behind him were two other men in denim work clothes; one carried a rifle.

"I am Captain Shaheed," he said, "and you are?"

"I am called Serb."

"Well, Serb, I understand that you have some cargo for me?"

"That is correct," Serb replied. "Twelve small crates."

"Very well. My men will rig a hoist at the rail, and we can haul them aboard."

Shaheed turned to the two men with him and began issuing orders in a language that Serb didn't know, but thought was probably Arabic. They left, and returned shortly with other men and the hoist equipment. In fifteen minutes, the first of the crates was coming aboard the yacht. In another twenty-five minutes, all twelve were aboard.

Shaheed issued another order, and one his men scuffled off. A few minutes later, the largest man that Serb had ever seen, walked, or rather waddled, toward them on deck. He wore all white: white suit, white tie, white shoes, white yacht cap. His face, Serb noted, was puffy, florid, with a small mouth and nose, and small pig eyes. It was Anubis Cline.

"You are late," the man said, in English.

"No help for it," Serb replied. "We had to take care of some business, an American policeman who was stowed away on our boat."

"Vitelli? Not Vitelli, was it?"

"The very same. But he will cause trouble no longer. Vitelli sleeps with the fishes."

Cline let out a satisfied grunt, his version of a triumphant laugh.

"You are Reaper?" Serb enquired.

"I am. You have my paintings?" he asked.

"I do," Serb answered. "See for yourself."

"Oh, I shall," Cline said, and nodded to Shaheed, who moved toward the crates on cue.

Shaheed noted that the crates were just as Cline had said they would be: constructed so that simply by turning a few wing nuts, they could be opened, emptied, and refilled, with ease. He attacked the closest case; it was labeled "Matisse, Boston"

Minutes later, the contents of the crate were on display, and the large man became furious.

"What is the meaning of this?" he raged.

165

Gene Masters

Chapter 50

Across the lagoon from the *Isole di San Michele*, the island where Venetians bury their dead, on the *Fondamente dei Mendicanti*, is Venice's hospital, the *Ospedale Santi Giovanni e Paulo*, better known to the locals simply as the *Ospedale Civili*. The building's elaborate façade speaks to the fact that the building was once a fifteenth-century monastery.

Off the spacious and ornate grand entrance hall is a labyrinth of hallways and rooms housing the various services one would expect to find in any modern hospital: patient rooms, operating theatres, radiology centers, laboratories, administrative offices, an emergency room, intensive care, and so on.

At first light, the water ambulance, with Vitelli and Giudice aboard, arrived at the *Ospedale Civili* from the Arsenal Coast Guard Station. On admission, Vitelli was quickly treated for hypothermia and shock, and placed in intensive care.

Pam Vitelli, alerted by Matteo Giudice, was at the hospital almost before the water ambulance arrived. She waited in the entrance hall, and was soon joined by Giudice. "He is suffering from hypothermia and shock," he told her. "But they say his vital signs are strong, and he should recover. They have him in the intensive care, but say that is just a precaution." Pam was not at all relieved by that report, and dragged from Giudice what he knew about her husband ending up, bound hands and feet, aboard a skiff floating in the Adriatic Sea—which, in truth, was not much.

Pam and Matteo then waited together for further news.

A member of the hospital staff eventually sought them out, but could not give them any more information other than Vitelli was still in intensive care, that he had responded to treatment, but was out of immediate danger. The staff member advised them both to return home until the following morning, when Vitelli would probably be out of the ICU and assigned a regular room. Only then would they be able to see him.

Giudice, himself exhausted, decided to take that advice, and begged Pam to do likewise. But Pam insisted on staying, spending the rest of the day, and the following night, on an uncomfortable settee in the grand entrance hall.

Vitelli was awake and alert when she finally got to see him early that following morning. Grabbing his hand, Pam's first words to her husband were, "Matteo told me what you did, how you must have stowed away aboard that boat. What were you thinking? You almost got yourself killed!"

"I missed you, too," Vitelli replied, with a wan smile.

"That's not funny. I think I'd kill you myself for that dumbass play, if you hadn't almost died!"

"But I didn't," he said, "and you can thank my old friend Chuck."

"Chuck? Chuck who? What in heaven's name are you talking about?"

"Red Cross Chuck. Never knew his last name. Taught me to float."

"You're not making any sense. Dammit Richie, you scared the wits out of me!" and, uncharacteristically, Pam teared up.

"I'm so sorry, babe. Really. I don't know what made me jump on that boat, but I just did. And you're right, it was a dumbass play."

Pam responded by leaning over and embracing her husband. "Easy," he quipped, "I might break."

"I don't think so," she said, still teary-eyed.

"So, how's Cal Iams holding up? Have they found Donna's body yet?"

"Donna's body?" Pam said, taken aback. "Why Donna showed up at the Museum yesterday, a little disheveled, but just fine!"

"Great!" Vitelli said, happily surprised. "That little bastard on the boat—called himself Serb—told me that she'd been murdered, and that they threw her body into a canal."

"Well, she wasn't, and they didn't. She said the guy that was guarding her just left all the doors open in the house where they were keeping her, and took off without a word."

"Wonderful! But Serb—the head of the gang that stole the paintings—he had been so certain she was dead.

And then he almost certainly tried to kill me. But then Serb told me a lot of things — things I need to tell Matteo. You have to tell him. Tell Matteo I need to see him."

"Time enough for that later, and I'm sure he'll be around shortly. Meanwhile, you need to get some rest."

"No time for that," Vitelli said, as his eyes closed and he dozed off.

Chapter 51

In the early daylight, even Serb could see that something was wrong with the painting that had just been taken out of its crate. "They looked just fine last night," he pleaded.

"Just fine?!" the large man could barely spit out the words. "Fine? A fine *print* maybe, but certainly no original Matisse." He struggled to control his anger. Finally, he said, "Open the others, Captain."

When the contents of the other eleven crates were exposed, the man in white said Serb in disgust, "All prints! How could you not know that the paintings had been switched out on you?"

"They could not have been, Reaper. I opened and examined each one," he lied. "The light was not the best, and it was raining, but there were all the colors on the paper, just as they should have been, end even the brush strokes."

"High quality prints on embossed paper, you idiot, all nicely framed. The whole lot is worth maybe five hundred dollars! Go! Get out of my sight, before I have you shot."

"Wait a minute," Serb said, "I delivered on our part of the deal. I was given the twelve crates by the American, Iams, and they looked authentic enough. I am hardly an art expert, after all. But me and my people did our part. We abducted Iam's wife, stole and repainted that boat, took all the risks. We even killed two people to pull this off! You can't just dismiss me—us—without paying." He struggled to calm himself, to appear reasonable, then continued. "Charlie said there was to be a bank transfer—"

"A bank transfer? Pay you? For what? You did all you did for five-hundred-dollars' worth of prints! I can assure you I have already wasted far more than five hundred measly dollars on this misadventure already. I will not throw good money after bad. What I will do is throw you off this ship! Now go, while you're still breathing."

Serb had enough sense to scramble back down the Jacob's ladder and get back aboard the boat below.

Chapter 52

Later the same morning, Vitelli awoke from his nap refreshed and alert. Pam was still in the room, but she had been awake all of the day before and most of the night, and had just dozed off. But now there was also another visitor: Matteo Giudice.

"Matteo," Vitelli said, "I've got a lot to tell you."

"Take it easy," Giudice said. "You have had a near thing. Better you should rest a bit and conserve your energy."

"I'm fine," Vitelli insisted. "I just had a really good nap, and I feel fine."

"Very well. But you must stop if you start feeling tired."

Instead, Vitelli jumped right in. "Serb, the man on the fishing boat, thought he was talking to a dead man. He told me some things he might not have told me otherwise."

"Serb? He was definitely one of the two men who abducted *Signora* Iams. She identified him from his what-you-call 'mugshot.' He and another man called Hulk, but she could not identify him from the pictures."

"Yes, well Serb was definitely in charge of the thugs aboard that fishing boat, I can tell you, and it was he and his gang that actually stole the paintings. Before the paintings were loaded aboard the boat, I even watched him order Cal Iams around, and pull three of the paintings out of their crates to ensure they were authentic."

"Did he now? Inspect them, did he?" To Vitelli, Giudice seemed amused. But Vitelli went on. "Yes. And when they were busy, I snuck aboard the boat, hiding in some sort of locker in the stern. Long story short, once we got out to sea, I was discovered and tied up. Look, Matteo, they knew there was a transmitter planted in with the paintings! Who knew that? Just you and me, right? We never told Iams."

"No, only the two of us and Captain Benedetto knew about the transmitter."

"Okay. Benedetto, too, then. Well, somehow, Serb and his crew knew about it. I'm thinking the guy Serb called Charlie — the person here in Venice he worked directly for — found out about it somehow." Vitelli paused, perhaps to let that bit of information stew in Giudice's mind for a few seconds.

"Before they tossed me overboard (Pam, now awake, and listening to their conversation, shuddered), Serb told me that this Charlie guy planned the entire heist. It was this Charlie person that had Donna Iams abducted, and it was Charlie that made all the plans for the actual theft of the paintings." Another pause; Vitelli just catching his breath.

"But get this. Charlie was not the mastermind. The mastermind, who calls himself Reaper, was an American. It was this Reaper who bankrolled the whole operation. He was waiting for the paintings to be delivered where the boat was headed — Trieste. Apparently, he had

arranged for sale of the paintings on the black market—
had buyers all lined up."

"I thought it might be something like that," Giudice
said, brow knit, taking it all in.

"By the way," Vitelli asked, "What ever happened to
those policemen who were supposed to be stationed at
the museum that night? You know they never showed
up, right?"

"I do." Giudice said.

"And?"

"And Captain Benedetto said afterward that he had
left specific written instructions to station the men at the
museum. I distinctly remember him telling me that he
would do that—and that he wanted me on that lighter."

"You did say that," Vitelli agreed. "And?"

"And it seems that somehow those 'specific written
instructions' never got delivered to the Sergeant who was
supposed to be in charge of the contingent."

"So, then, all it took was three thieves and a boat, and
millions of dollars in artwork gets stolen. It seems to me
your Captain has a lot to answer for," Vitelli said.

"Perhaps. But the artwork was never stolen."

"What?"

"The crates were filled with prints. Iams switched
out the real paintings and substituted prints."

Vitelli was flabbergasted. "You're serious?"

"I am."

"Iams did that?"

"He did."

"Wow. I'm blown away. Iams? Who'd of thought he had the balls to do something like that? Not with them holding Donna!"

"I talked to him about that, and he blames you."

"What? Me? I'd never, ever, have told him to pull a switch like that."

"Perhaps. But you did convince him that once the thieves got their hands on the paintings, *Signora* Iams fate was sealed one way or another. They would either kill her, or turn her loose, and that it was all determined *before* the theft actually took place. I think he figured he really had nothing to lose by switching out the paintings."

"Then it was a close thing when Serb inspected those three paintings. If he knew anything about that kind of art, there would have been hell to pay."

"Indeed. Iams said he was grateful for the poor lighting on the dock, the rain, and the quality of the prints."

"But those odds don't sound all that great to me. Even given it *was* Serb doing the inspecting, he was taking quite a chance."

"Perhaps. But you also said that Serb told you that Donna Iams had been killed."

"He did. And he sounded dead certain. And he was certainly willing enough to have me dumped into the drink and drown, so I believed him. Somehow, and for whatever reason, whomever was supposed to actually murder Donna Iams must have backed out."

"I agree. I have an idea it was the man called 'Hulk,' given what I suspect was the *Signora's* reluctance to pick out his mugshot."

"You did say that she picked out Serb, but not Hulk," Vitelli said, recalling that information.

"Exactly. Well, anyway, we did convince her to show us where they were holding her prisoner. Took her a bit of backtracking to find it, but find it she did. The place, some upper rooms over a store in the Cannaregio, was vacant. But some of the thieves' stuff, like cooking equipment and bedding, was still there. Captain Benedetto agreed to get a team to watch the place, just in case they return. We do not have the manpower at *San Marco*, so he arranged it with the commandant of the command station in Cannaregio, *Comandante* Rubio, for the what-do-you-call 'stakeout.'"

"I don't think there's much chance of the thieves returning, but it's certainly worth a try," Vitelli opined.

"Never say never, my friend. Who would have thought, after all, that Serb and his crew calmly tied up Iams and the museum guards, while not three meters away from them the real artwork was stacked, just leaning against the wall?"

"Yeah," Vitelli grinned, "who'd have thought?"

Vitelli was released from the hospital that afternoon.

Chapter 53

I am, my dear, surrounded by fools.

The yacht formerly identified as "Zayed," now with a different name and port city freshly painted on her stern, made its way down the Adriatic and toward the Mediterranean. Its destination was its actual home port in Palma, Majorca. Now, Anubis Cline held another imaginary conversation with his deceased ward, Jael.

"How is that, Abba?"

I paid a pretty penny to set up the greatest art theft of the century, and employed what promised to be a skilled, and well-connected, team of professionals to pull it off. My plan was essentially flawless, but was foiled in the end by the simplest of deeds – switching out worthless prints for the actual paintings. Now I must explain to my waiting clients that the artwork I had promised will never be delivered.

"But some of them helped fund the project, did they not?"

They did indeed. And they will be the most displeased. Now I must make good their investment, as well as explain my incompetence.

"Who could have switched out the paintings, Abba?"

Only one person – Calvin Iams. It had to be him. No one else had the access, time, or opportunity.

"But his wife was being held hostage, was she not?"

She was indeed. I had been so certain that, with his wife held captive, Iams would not only cooperate, but facilitate, the theft! Someone must have convinced him otherwise.

"And who might that have been, Abba?"

Vitelli. It had to be. He must have convinced Iams that his wife's fate had already been determined. That her eventual life or death had nothing to do with whether or not he delivered the paintings into our hands.

"And had it, Abba?"

Had it what, Jael?

"Had the Iams woman's fate already been determined?"

I suppose so. Probably. I did not know nor did I care, really. The Iams woman may indeed have been killed – or released – it was no matter to me. She was Charlie's problem, and I had advised Charlie, in any case, to look to it: to neutralize either the Iams woman, or her abductors. The only positive development from this whole mess is that I will never again have to deal with Vitelli – not ever again.

"Yes, there is that. But back to what matter – the shipment. You arranged that the shipment be inspected in Venice, even before it was loaded abord the boat, did you not?"

I most certainly did. It's pathetic that that cretin Serb could not distinguish between the paintings and mere prints.

"Obviously a man devoid of any artistic knowledge."

Yes. And I blame Charlie for that. It was Charlie who recruited him and his gang.

"And what now, Abba? Do we just return the yacht to its owner in Majorca, and fly home with our tail between our legs?"

Of course not, Jael. Cline laughed aloud, or rather he grunted aloud, which, for him, was a full-throated laugh.

Of course not! I have already taken steps to minimize the damage. Charlie and the incompetents Charlie hired will have to work out among themselves their financial shortfall — the result of their own incompetence. That, for them, will be punishment enough. But Calvin Iams — it had to be Iams who substituted those prints for the real paintings — he will feel my displeasure, that much I assure you!

"I do not doubt that for a minute, Abba."

Chapter 54

Serb and his men drove the sport fisher back to Venice, and entered the lagoon by the Malamocco Inlet. They abandoned the stolen craft by the dock at Porto Marghera, just a little over three kilometers from the city.

It had never occurred to Serb that it might be too dangerous to return to Venice; he had been in far more dangerous situations in the past and had always managed to prevail. No, he and his gang had been promised a hundred thousand euros for their part in this little adventure, and he intended to collect that money. He, of course, would keep most of it, but, Hulk, Marco, and his other team member, Giulio, who had served as the boat's helmsman, they deserved their share of that money. Charlie had promised them that money, and now Serb and his gang were coming to collect.

Never mind that Reaper, the huge man in the white suit, stiffed Charlie. That's between White Suit and Charlie, Serb thought. He and his men had done exactly as they had been ordered. *We abducted and imprisoned the old lady, stole the fishing boat and repainted it, stole the paintings, and delivered them to that yacht in Trieste, just like Charlie ordered. Never mind that we also had to get rid of two witnesses in the process—that Iams woman and the American cop. No, we earned that money, and now I mean to collect!*

Charlie could hardly blame them for what that little prick Iams, did. *It had to have been Iams who switched out the paintings. Probably made his own deal to sell them on the side. If he's still in the city, I'll find him and kill him, just like we did his old lady!*

BACK IN THE CITY, Serb and his two men waited until the middle of the night—the wee hours of Wednesday morning—before they made their way on foot to their old hideout: the place in the Cannaregio where they had held the Iams woman. There Serb fully expected to find Hulk waiting there.

They approached the building warily. No telling what might have happened while they were out of town—not that anything should have happened; with the old lady dead, Serb and Hulk were in the clear. At that hour, there wasn't a soul on the street, and everything appeared to be quiet. Still, the three men couldn't help but creep stealthily along, staying in the shadows as much as possible. When they finally reached the door, and went inside the building, they didn't switch on the hallway lights. Instead, they waited in the hallway for their eyes to adjust to the dark before ascending the stairs to the floor where Serb and Hulk had been living, and where Donna Iams had been held.

Once upstairs, still in the dark, Serb called out in a loud whisper, *"Hulk, sei gui?"* (Hulk, are you in here?)

No answer.

Serb crept to the room where Hulk and he had slept. Only then did he turn on the light. The room was clean, the bed made, and none of Hulk's stuff—not that there

184

had been much—was there. "Huh!" Serb grunted, puzzled that his henchman had cleared out.

Suddenly, all was pandemonium. It sounded like a herd of shouting oxen was coming up the stairs, all carrying bright lights. Serb considered making his way to a window and jumping out, and was actually on his way to do just that, when he was fixed in a light beam. *"Non muoverti!"* (Don't move!) the man shouted. *"Polizia!"* Serb knew enough to throw up his hands and freeze.

Chapter 55

"Don't you dare have second thoughts about it!" Donna Iams scolded her husband. "You did exactly the right thing! You've got to stop beating yourself up!"

"But what if I had been wrong?" Cal Iams replied. "After all, you were still very much alive. What if that ugly little man had been smarter, and realized that I had switched out the paintings?"

"And if he had, so what? Rich Vitelli told you that that 'ugly little man,' as you call him — this Serb character — was sure his partner had already killed me and dumped me in a canal. He told Rich that I was dead even before he stole what he thought were the originals! Would you feel better about taking that chance, and switching out the paintings, if Serb's partner had actually gone ahead and killed me?"

"God, no! How could you think such a thing?"

"I don't, you idiot. But I'm also glad you saved the paintings. And you did, you know. Because the delivery to Trieste was actually made! Had it been the originals, it would have been the art theft of the century! And you would have been held responsible! As it was, they went through a whole lot of trouble for nothing. I would have loved to have been there when the mastermind that arranged it all, found out that the switch had been made!"

Iams chuckled. Donna was right. That had to have been a sight to see!

"And as for my not being murdered," Donna continued, "I'm willing to bet that was no fault of this Serb character. He would have ordered the other one, the man he called Hulk, to do the deed. And apparently it was an order that the kindly Giorgio simply couldn't carry out. God bless him, poor man! He was really quite a gentle person once you got to know him, you know?"

"He was a kidnapper and a thief, Donna."

"Yes. Perhaps he was. But he was no murderer."

Chapter 56

It was Wednesday morning, and the Vitellis had already delayed their return home at the request of the Venetian authorities. Vitelli was concerned about the reception he would get from Captain Parker, back in the city. He could just hear him: "Having too good a time on your European vacation to come back and go to work, were you?"

Then there was also the additional drain on his pocketbook to consider.

Giudice met Vitelli as he entered the St. Mark's Station. "We need to talk, Rich," he said, and he ushered him into the office.

"Hello to you, too," scoffed Vitelli. "And where is the fair Sergeant Capello this morning? Not on duty today? She is far more welcoming than you are!"

"Carlotta called in sick this morning. I am a bit worried about her. But come, I have reserved an interview room for us to use."

Vitelli sat down with Giudice in a separate second-floor room at the San Marco police station, a room thankfully insulated from the goings-on in the rest of the station.

"You look concerned—worried—about something, Matteo, what is it?"

"I have been thinking, and it all fits. I think Captain Benedetto, is this, what-do-you-call, 'facilitator,' the man called Charlie—the one who hired Serb's gang, and did all the planning."

"I doubt that, Matteo," Vitelli said.

"You do not think Captain Benedetto is this facilitator, the man pulling the strings here in *Venezia,* Rich? After all, how obvious can it be? The man's name *is* Carlo, so the American what-do-you-call, 'mastermind'—this American 'Reaper' person—would, of course, call him 'Charlie.'"

"Yeah, I know," Vitelli replied, "but that's way too easy. Just too obvious. Anybody can call themselves by any name they want. And Benedetto—he's due to retire soon, isn't he?"

"He is."

"And he has how many years on the force?"

"Twenty-four, I think, or something such as that. He could certainly retire anytime he wanted to. He has already earned a generous pension."

"And why would he jeopardize all of that?"

"Because those paintings were worth millions?"

"To whomever sells them, the guy who calls himself Reaper. The facilitator only gets peanuts in comparison, even though he takes all the risks."

"All right. But, still, it was the captain who ordered me to be on that lighter, away from all the action, and it was he who was supposed to have ordered the men to be on the dock at the time of the theft. Remember? The policemen who never showed up?"

"Okay, but both of you thought there was a good chance the thieves planned to take over the lighter and use it to transport the paintings. That didn't happen, but it was certainly a logical enough scenario. And you did say he issued a written order to deploy the men."

"He *says* he did. I asked him about it again yesterday. He said he issued the order for Sergeant Montebello. He was to be in charge of an armed force made up of himself and four men. And they were to be on the Accademia dock before midnight Sunday last. But I asked him, and Montebello said he never saw any such order."

"And why a *written* order? Why not just tell him directly?"

"Two reasons, apparently. Benedetto's wife became ill, and he wanted to go home to her, and Montebello had not yet started his shift."

"Sounds reasonable enough, just find that written order."

"That is a problem. It seems to have disappeared."

"How could that have happened?"

"Good question. One explanation is that no such order was ever issued."

"That might be hard to prove," Vitelli ventured.

Giudice shrugged, then said, "There is also the matter about the transmitter."

"Yes, there is that," Vitelli agreed.

"Exactly. Only three of us knew about it—you, me, and the captain. Yet somehow the thieves knew all about it too—as you yourself observed."

"Again, true. But there is always the possibility that somebody else knew about it."

"I told no one. Did you?"

"No. Not Iams, not my wife."

"Well, then?"

"But Benedetto may have told someone else. You could ask him."

"Then he would know that we suspect him. Everything we have now is merely, what-do-you-call, 'circumstantial?' What we must do now is question this Serb character. He will know who this facilitator is."

He might indeed, Vitelli mused. *Bet he'll be surprised to see me!*

Chapter 57

Carlo Benedetto was unhappy about Giudice's insistence that Vitelli sit in on the Serb's questioning, but he relented when his junior officer reminded him that Serb had been sure that Vitelli was dead, that Vitelli's appearance at the questioning might just rattle the thief enough for him to give a full confession.

"If Benedetto was Charlie, then he would have fought tooth and nail to keep me away from the questioning," Vitelli said to Giudice before Serb was brought into the interview room for questioning. They were in the main police headquarters in the Cannaregio section of the city, where the men who had captured him and his two compatriots were stationed.

The setup, Vitelli noted, was very much like the interrogation rooms back in his home city: small, brightly lit room, video camera recording the interview, a table and some chairs, the see-through mirror behind which Benedetto and his boss, the Venetian Police Commander Rubio would observe. Vitelli and Giudice were seated opposite Serb when he was brought in and seated with his hands shackled to the table.

If Serb was surprised to see Vitelli, he hid it well. His pockmarked face was in a fixed sneer as he said in

English, "Well! I see our American friend managed to get rescued. Enjoy your swim, cop?"

"Not nearly as much as I will see you going down for murdering Donna Iams and for my attempted murder, Mister Ilić," Vitelli answered, taking the chance that Serb did not know that Donna Iams was still alive.

"So, you have done your homework, have you? Congratulations. You know my real name. I still prefer Serb. And I did not murder *Signora* Iams. Hulk did that. And since you are still alive, it is obvious that I murdered no one. All me and my boys did was transport some copies of famous paintings to a yacht called *Zayed* docked in Trieste."

So, he doesn't know Donna Iams is still alive. He thinks he can't go down for abducting her! We can use that, Vitelli mused.

"What is obvious, *Signore* Ilić," Giudice began, "Is that you have to be the world's worst art thief. All that abduction, murder, and attempted murder for what? Twelve quality art prints?"

Serb squirmed, but stayed silent.

"You even had the chance to discover that *Signore* Iams had switched out the real paintings," Giudice continued, "and you were unable to tell the difference, even after you examined three of them."

"So? All you can prove so far is that I am no art expert. Besides, the lighting on the dock was very poor. And it was raining. They were only globs of color after all, those wonderful artworks, now, were they not?"

"Perhaps. But the originals were worth millions. I do not imagine the person you delivered the painting to was very happy about that. What did you call him? Reaper?" Giudice asked.

"Yes, him!" Serb seethed at the memory. "Big fat bastard in a white suit on a big fancy yacht! That bastard had to weigh one-hundred-seventy kilos if he weighed a gram."

Vitelli's mind reeled. *A big fat man in a white suit? It can't be. But who else could it be? Anubis Cline! Cline is Reaper? He was behind all this? Can't be! Here in Italy?*

"Tell me, Serb," Vitelli broke in, "this big guy in the white suit, what'd he look like?"

"As I said. Dressed in white from head to toe. Ugly. Face all round and puffed up, you know? Tiny, nasty eyes. Shuffled side to side when he walked."

"Could you identify him? Say, from a photograph?"

"Probably," Serb replied. "If it was worth something to me."

Cline, you bastard! We may just have you now! Vitelli sat back, obviously lost in thought. Giudice resumed the questioning.

"Very well, Mister Ilić, so much for this mastermind, Reaper, on the yacht in Trieste. Let us talk about the person you called the facilitator — this Charlie — the man who directed your operation here in *Venezia*."

Serb sneered, his face wrapped in an evil smile.

"What?" Giudice asked. "What did I say so that was so amusing?"

"Nothing." Serb was obviously lying, and both Vitelli and Giudice knew it, but not about what. Giudice continued the questioning.

"This facilitator—Charlie, you called him—the one who directed you and Hulk to kidnap Donna Iams—"

"Wait a minute," Serb interrupted. "I had nothing to do with that, and you cannot prove that I did!"

"Oh, but we can Mister Ilić," Giudice smiled, "You see, Donna Iams is still very much alive. And she has already identified you from your arrest photo as one of the two men that abducted her."

"But Hulk . . ." Serb began, and then thought better of it.

"Is nowhere to be found," Giudice said, finishing Serb's thought. "Now. Once more. It was this Charlie that directed you to abduct *Signora* Iams?"

"Yes."

"Charlie told you to kill her?"

"Said she could identify us, Hulk and me. Blow the whole operation."

"And was it Charlie who told you about the transmitter hidden in with the paintings?"

"Yes."

"Tell me, Mister Ilić, this Charlie, can you identify him?"

"Yes," he said laughing.

"What is so amusing?" Giudice demanded.

"You," he replied. "Charlie, you see, is not a man. Charlie is a woman!"

Chapter 58

Giudice and Vitelli were back at St. Mark's station.

"Yes, Matteo, I'm pretty certain that the man Serb calls Reaper, the mastermind behind this whole caper is a man named Anubis Cline. It should be easy enough to download his picture off the Internet, and show it to Serb for positive identification."

"Well, if it was this Cline person aboard the yacht, he is no longer in Trieste. The port director there said the *Zayed* left port sometime during the night. The Coast Guard has been alerted, but they are few, and there are many yachts in the Mediterranean."

"No matter. If I know Cline, he's already on his way back to the States. But with Serb's identification, you can extradite the bastard and bring him to trial. Besides conspiracy to steal the paintings, there are also two attempted murders."

"If this Cline is our man, then I am not so sure that Serb's testimony will be sufficient to get him extradited from the States. We need to find this Charlie person."

Vitelli had already decided, now that they knew Charlie was a woman, that the most likely candidate for 'this Charlie person,' was Carlotta Capello. Now he had to clear up a few loose ends, and then convince Giudice that Carlotta was Charlie.

"You asked Captain Benedetto about that lost written order for Sergeant Montebello?"

"I did," Giudice answered. "He said he was in a hurry to go home to his wife. He did not want to wait until Montebello came in for his shift, so he gave it to Carlotta to give to him."

"So, she could have just tossed it. And she called in sick again this morning?"

"No, she did not. But I looked for her, and she did not come in this morning either. I tried calling her, but her phone is shut off. I think perhaps she is just home resting, and does not want to be disturbed."

"Then maybe you should go to her place and check on her."

"I could, if I knew where it was."

"Your own girlfriend, and you don't know where she lives?"

"No. We always arranged just to meet somewhere. To keep it quiet that we were dating, you know? And she was not the kind of a girlfriend you might be thinking of, anyway. We had not been dating that long, and had just been getting to know each other."

"Okay." *So, they haven't been intimate.* "How about getting her address from personnel?"

"Not a good idea. That is personal information, and I would need a good reason to ask. She does not report to me, after all, but to the captain."

"Okay, but you just might have a very good reason to ask," Vitelli said. "Sergeant Capello — Carlotta — was in a position to know all about the operation. That you have to admit. Only thing that doesn't fit is that transmitter.

To be Charlie, she would have to have known about it. Is it possible Benedetto told her?"

"No. He was upset with me that I asked, too, but he assured me that he told no one else about the transmitter."

"Okay. But before we accuse and convict her, how about you get that address from personnel, and we go check on her, see what she has to say."

"Okay. We go now."

Chapter 59

Leaving the borrowed Yacht in Mallorca, Anubis Cline boarded a borrowed private jet at *Aeroporto Palma de Mallorca*. The airplane, a Dassault Falcon 8X, could easily take off and land on the Palma airport's limited runways, and was one of the few that could make the trip direct to Long Island's MacArthur Airport without refueling. After topping off there, the plane would fly to the city, where Cline's specially-equipped Lincoln was parked and waiting for him to drive it home.

Cline was the plane's sole passenger, unless one counted the solid gold urn that contained his ward's ashes, which was securely strapped into the seat opposite his. If the lovely Chinese stewardess thought that that was at all strange, she managed to hide it well from the super-sized man in the white linen suit.

"Are you sure, sir? All you will require is green tea?" she asked Cline in perfect English, once the plane was in the air.

"Quite sure," Cline answered. "Airplane's give me a queasy stomach, and the tea is calming."

"Very well, sir," she said and shuffled off to brew the tea.

Cline mulled over his European experience, discussing it in his mind's eye with the passenger sitting opposite from him.

Not our finest hour, was it, Jael, Cline started matter-of-factly.

"No, Abba, it was not, although, at least, you were careful with your arrangements not to leave any loose ends behind."

Yes, I was. Suspicion and conjecture can abound, but they cannot convict. Only solid evidence can do that. I have managed in the past, my dear, to avoid indictment, much less conviction, and I intend to continue to do so in the future. So, all solid evidence must be disposed of.

"As to solid evidence, Abba, this Charlie, she is no threat to us?"

Not at all. All my dealings with her were at arm's length. Our only method of contact was by satellite telephone, and the one I used to contact her with is now at the bottom of the Mediterranean. I threw it overboard, just as I ordered those prints to be thrown overboard. I'm sorry they only floated, but, still, they floated away, and there is no way to connect them to us. I am still amazed that Calvin Iams had the intestinal fortitude to switch them for the original paintings.

"Yes, one would have thought that he would not have been willing to put the life of his wife at risk. Something, or someone, must have convinced him otherwise."

Someone indeed. I suspect that the late Detective Vitelli convinced Iams that his wife would be killed, no matter what he did. No matter. There is plenty of time to make Iams suffer even more for ruining my little enterprise.

"And we are sure that Detective Vitelli is dead?"

We have the Serb's testimony that he was drowned in the Adriatic. And with Vitelli dead, then there is at least one positive thing that resulted from this whole affair.

Cline took note that now his ward remained strangely silent. It was as if she knew something he didn't.

"I have your tea, sir," the stewardess said, disturbing his reverie.

Chapter 60

The late morning sun was bright above, and there wasn't a cloud in the sky. But it was Autumn, after all, and the air was crisp and cool. Ideal weather for an expeditionary stroll to the place where Carlotta Capello said she lived.

"Are you sure this is the right address, Matteo?" Vitelli asked.

"Positive. This is the correct street, and that is the correct number."

"But it's an antique shop. Nobody lives here. Is this where they were mailing Carlotta's paychecks?"

"Where have you been, Rich? Nobody gets paychecks mailed anymore. Everything is direct deposit."

"Yeah, so is my paycheck, come to think of it. And my guess now is that if you check on the account where her checks have been deposited, you may well find it has been cleaned out. She's gone, Matteo, flown the coop. Nobody innocent just takes off like that. The only thing that doesn't add up is the transmitter. To be Charlie, she had to have known about that. Matteo, tell me, where did the transmitter come from?"

"I bought it. I found it in a little security shop on the Giudecca. They sell things like cameras and microphones. The one I bought was designed to attach to a motor vehicle so as to trace it. The locals use it on their boats. I thought it was just the thing."

"And it was. It pretty much saved my life. Who knew you were going there and why?"

"Well, Carlotta was with me at the time. But I'm certain she had no idea why we were there."

"Did she know what you bought?"

"She probably heard me asking about a transmitter, but she had no idea what it was for — she could not have."

"So. But she knew you bought a transmitter."

"All right. But not why, or what for."

"Okay. But she could have easily figured that out," Vitelli gently suggested.

"Maybe. But I do not think that is highly likely. In the end, only three of us knew what the transmitter was *really* for."

"Come on, Matteo. You know very well she could have figured it out."

A crestfallen Giudice finally said, "It *is* possible."

Chapter 61

That afternoon, when Pam and Rich were in their hotel room, and she had heard Vitelli's narrative of the morning's adventures with Giudice, Pam said, "Fine. You go interviewing crooks and antique shopping with your policeman buddy, and leave me here to pack for the trip home! Is this what the rest of our married life is going to be like?"

"I'm sorry, hon', but we only stayed on here so the police could tie up the loose ends."

He went on to bring her up to speed on the case: Serb's testimony; Charlie being a woman; Carlotta Capello most likely being Charlie; and Anubis Cline being Reaper, the mastermind behind the whole affair.

"Wow," she said, "you boys have been busy! And poor Matteo! He had a thing for that girl, Carlotta."

Vitelli grinned, feeling vindicated for having had to desert his wife all morning. "He'll survive. I got the distinct impression that their relationship was not all that far along."

"Well," she said, "I have a bit of news of my own. I peed on a stick this morning."

"You what?'

"Peed on a stick. A home pregnancy test? They have them here in Italy too, you know."

"What test was that?"

"Pregnancy, Rich. The stick came up positive. You're going to be a father."

"What? When? I'm going to be a *father*?"

"Looks like it. Test is supposed to be ninety-nine-per-cent accurate."

"Woo Hoo! Yippee!"

Then Vitelli did a silly thing: He grabbed his wife and danced with her around the room.

Chapter 62

Carlotta Capello sat in her uninspiring room in a two-star hotel on the outskirts of Milan.

It had been, she had to admit, an interesting ride. She had been stuck in go-nowhere, just-smile-and-be-pretty jobs ever since she graduated from the police academy. Italian police departments, despite the promises they had made when they recruited her for the program, were very much boys' clubs. Venice St. Mark's Station had been no different. So, when she was cruising the dark web, and ran across Reaper's post, she thought *Why not? Why not answer the ad? What have I got to lose?*

As it turned out, the answer was pretty much every-thing.

The attraction was, of course, the money. Carlotta was well aware that the paintings she would scheme to steal were worth millions. She also knew well she would see only a fraction of that, even if their scheme had come off without a hitch. Reaper, after all, had the contacts to sell the paintings, and then only for less than half of their real value. He would get the lion's share of the proceeds.

Still, what Carlotta—Charlie—would clear was quite substantial, even if she paid off the team she would as-semble to actually pull off the heist.

It was Reaper who had arranged for her to set up a numbered account at that bank in San Marino. The principality, an independent state totally inside Italy, was a mere hundred and sixty kilometers away from Venice — a day trip by train. In a numbered account, the identity of the holder is replaced with a multi-digit number, a number known only to the client and selected private bankers.

Reaper had assured her that the seed money for their little scheme was waiting for her in San Marino. She had only to go there in person and open the account, and that only she would know the account number. She could then deposit the money waiting there in the account that only she cold access.

Once at the bank, the banker who helped her open the account, the dapper *Signore* Tedesco, assured her that *Signore* Reaper had been correct, and that only a person knowing the account number had access to the account. He also verified that she would be the only one who knew that number. So, Carlotta opened the account, and somehow, a quarter million euros suddenly appeared in it.

She withdrew just enough to cover operating expenses, and then some; but there was still a hundred and seventy thousand euros left in the account.

Once the paintings were delivered, Reaper would deposit another half million.

Even considering operating expenses, Carlotta figured that if everything went according to plan, she would clear six hundred and fifty thousand, easy — especially since she callously planned to stiff Serb and his team, and keep their share of the payout for herself.

Six hundred and fifty thousand euros. On her Sergeant's pay, it would take her over seventeen years to earn that much — and by then she would be old and fat.

CARLOTTA WAS ALREADY ON her way back to San Marino on Sunday, long before the action at the Oppenheim played out, and the paintings would be on their way to Reaper in Trieste. Her part was finished. She regretted that she had to order the old woman's death, but Reaper was right: she could identify Serb and Hulk. It was important that Serb, at least, trust that Charlie had had their best interests at heart. Team dedication is important. Police training had taught her that.

Cline, aboard the borrowed yacht, had already left Trieste, and was headed to the Mediterranean when Carlotta entered the bank with the intention of draining her numbered account, leaving Italy, and heading for America, the land of opportunity.

She had considered the possibility that Reaper, being a crook, would take possession of the paintings and never deposit the promised additional half million euros. But she really had no choice but to trust him to follow through on his end of the deal. If he did stiff her, all she could do was, anonymously, reveal to the media just how the paintings were stolen, and where they went. That would, at least, make the artwork harder for Reaper to sell. Not much of a plan, of course, but it was all she could come up with.

She was met at the bank on Tuesday morning by the same little impeccably dressed man who had helped her sign in for her account to begin with: *Signore* Tedesco. He sat her across from him at his carved mahogany desk in his glassed-in office and asked, in English, how he might again help her.

"I'm here about my account," she said.

"Of course. Tell me your account number, please."

Carlotta rattled off a string of eight numbers, while Tedesco entered them into a computer terminal. "Yes," he said, "here we are. Now how can I help you?"

"There should have been a large deposit yesterday," she said.

"I'm sorry, Miss Capello. There was no deposit— none at all in fact, for some time."

"You have the right account?" She rattled off the numbers again.

"Yes, Miss, this is the right account."

Damn, Carlotta thought, *that bastard Reaper* did *stiff me!* "Very well, then," she said, regaining her composure, "I wish to withdraw the remaining funds in the account." *One hundred and seventy thousand is better than nothing!*

"There must be some mistake, Miss Capello, all the remaining funds were withdrawn yesterday. One hundred and seventy thousand euros, and the interest earned, another forty-five."

"I don't understand," an astonished Carlotta said. "I understood that my number was required to withdraw *any* funds from the account, and that only I knew that number."

"You are correct, Miss. It was that number that was used yesterday to withdraw the remaining funds."

"But doesn't that have to be done in person?"

"Only if the withdrawal is in cash or check. Electronic transfer from one account to another, even to another bank, can be done by wire. All one would need is the proper numbers."

A stunned Carlotta left the bank empty handed. Somehow Reaper had gamed the system and had cleaned her out. She still had what was left of her first withdrawal, but it wasn't all that much, and wouldn't take her very far—certainly not to America.

All she knew for sure was that she could not go back to Venice. No matter. There was nothing more there for her anyway. That afternoon she took the train to Milan. There she would regroup, and see if there was any way to glean at least something from all this mess.

Now she sat in an uninspiring room in a two-star hotel on the outskirts of Milan, still wondering what she was going to do with the rest of her life.

Chapter 63

Vitelli's hopes of nailing Anubis Cline for kidnapping and attempted murder were quashed when the only person who could identify the person called Reaper, one Felip Ilić, died from a broken neck, the injury resulting from a fall in prison.

It seems that Ilić was on the second tier of an open prison court when he either fell, or was pushed, over the guardrail to the concrete floor below. An investigation of the incident by prison staff resulted in no explanation whatever for his fall. None of Ilić's fellow inmates, apparently, had seen a thing. His death was eventually officially ruled an accident by the prison officials.

THE TWELVE CRATES CONTAINING the art prints washed up on the shores of North Africa, one in Libya, the rest in Tunisia. The prints, of course, were ruined. Of those crates that were discovered and examined, only the crates themselves were salvaged, and then so that the wood could be dried and reused.

About the Author

Gene Masters is a retired consulting engineer living in East Tennessee with his wife, Ruth. They have two grown daughters, and two grandchildren. He is the author of several technical treatises, including his doctoral dissertation, and seven novels.

Masters received a commission in the U.S. Navy on graduation from Notre Dame, and his first tour of duty was aboard a transport in the Western Pacific. His second tour was aboard a recommissioned and updated diesel-electric submarine, the USS *Angler*, which was originally commissioned in 1943, and made seven war patrols in the Pacific before being decommissioned. Her updating to an SSK-class boat in the 1950s fitted her for operation against cold war submarine adversaries with advanced soundproofing and sonar. Masters left *Angler* and active duty after a Mediterranean tour. Later Naval Reserve assignments included the diesel-electric submarines USS *Manta* and the USS *Ling*.

After active duty, Masters pursued a career in engineering, and served in various companies until settling into a career as a consulting engineer. He retired in 2009. Readers can reach the author via email at 240boat@gmail.com, and view his website at *www.genemasters.net*.

A Word About Reviews

Reviews are the lifeblood of any author. If you enjoyed this book, would you please be kind enough to post a review wherever you think it might be helpful.

Thanks in advance!

Gene

www.ingramcontent.com/pod-product-compliance
Lightning Source LLC
Chambersburg PA
CBHW020328200626
46814CB00006BB/2475